## A kiss to build a dream on?

Rogan slid his hand around the back of Samantha's neck, threading his fingers through her hair and capturing her. She didn't want to escape.

Their lips fused and she didn't know whether she or Rogan had closed the final, minuscule gap between them. She knew only that it was his heat she wanted, his taste she craved.

She swayed into his embrace. He pulled her closer. Her heart beat faster and she could hardly breathe. She'd never wanted, needed, desired anyone the way she wanted Rogan. With a jagged breath, he drew back. He gripped her by the shoulders. "Ah, Carrot Top...there's something I've got to tell you...."

Samantha reached up to touch his lips, gently, her heart swelling with anticipation. "What's that?"

"When I fix you up with a guy, hold back on the first kiss. You don't want to give him too much all at once."

## ABOUT THE AUTHOR

Married with two adult, married daughters, Charlotte lives in Torrance, California. She is the author of more than a dozen American Romance novels and some Silhouette Romance books, as well. Charlotte is active in her community, and is best known for her weekly newspaper column, which has recruited 18,000 volunteers for 400 nonprofit organizations since 1969. Several of her recent books have made the Walden bestseller list. Charlotte loves to hear from readers, and can be reached at: P.O. Box 505, Torrance, CA 90508.

## Books by Charlotte Maclay

### HARLEQUIN AMERICAN ROMANCE

# CHARLOTTE MACLAY

## $TEALING $AMANTHA

# Harlequin Books

TORONTO • NEW YORK • LONDON
AMSTERDAM • PARIS • SYDNEY • HAMBURG
STOCKHOLM • ATHENS • TOKYO • MILAN
MADRID • WARSAW • BUDAPEST • AUCKLAND

Special thanks to Joan and Mindy.
As always, I couldn't have done it without you.

ISBN 0-373-16684-2

STEALING SAMANTHA

# Chapter One

A safecracker ought to be a middle-aged guy with a paunch and a lousy complexion. Or maybe a skinny cat burglar dressed in black.

The woman rifling the safe was neither of those.

*Vivid* came to mind. So did *knockout,* given the slinky sheath dress she was wearing, cut so low in back he could easily imagine the feminine swell of what little remained hidden. The combination of a vibrant green dress, soft-as-satin flesh and Orphan Annie tousled hair took his breath away. And the hair, at least, brought back memories.

Grinning, Rogan Prescott eased into the book-lined study and quietly closed the door behind him, shutting off the sound of music coming from downstairs. His host wouldn't be pleased to find one of his party guests rummaging through his safe, but Rogan was intrigued.

It took a lot to get him to take a second look these days. And this particular thief might be worth a third or fourth.

"Something I can help you find, Carrot Top?" he drawled.

Samantha Sterling froze.

She'd managed to get one hand on the jewelry box she'd discovered at the back of the safe and now she couldn't budge. She couldn't even breathe. She'd been nabbed the first time she'd cracked a safe. Talk about rotten luck. Everybody was supposed to be downstairs.

Worse, the idiot who had caught her had the nerve to call her *Carrot Top*. Lord, she hated that!

Grinding her teeth, Samantha decided she'd simply have to brazen her way through this awkward situation. She was desperately curious about the contents of that box, but now was not the time to press her luck.

As casually as she could manage, she released her grip on the velvet box, closed the safe door and spun the knob. Then she slid the oil painting of a seascape back into place to disguise the safe's location, although any child over six could have found it easily enough.

She lifted her chin, turned with a smile on her face, and then her heart did one of those weird stumbling beats that happen when you're shocked right out of your panty hose. Of all the men who might have caught her, why did it have to be him? Not that she hadn't seen Rogan Prescott's name on the invitation list. She might have even, on some subliminal level, hoped she'd have a chance to see him. But not this way.

*Or maybe, just maybe,* a perverse little voice in her head taunted, *you are here because you* hoped *you'd see him.*

He cocked his head, recognition slowly sinking into

his brilliant blue eyes along with a generous dose of incredulity. "Sam, is that you?"

"Hello, Rogan. It's been a long time. I'm surprised you remember me."

His gaze swept over her. Slowly. Starting at the top of her head, sliding across her face, then slipping with infinite care down the length of her body until her toes curled. "You've changed some," he conceded.

Sam cursed a complexion that verged on a blush under normal circumstances. After a look like that, her face was flaming. So were most of the other parts of her body.

Fingering the diamond teardrop earring she'd obtained on loan, she searched for a retort that would put him, not her, on the defensive. "Surely you're not so ungentlemanly as to suggest I was a little gangly when I was thirteen?" That had been the absolute truth ten years ago—the last time she'd seen Rogan— assuming he had even bothered to notice her.

"You aren't now." His lips curled into a familiar smile, all even white teeth and eyes crinkling at the corners, not to mention the crease of a dimple in his left cheek. "Very nice, Sam. You've grown up very nice indeed."

Maybe the gazillion hours she spent every week working out were worth it after all. "Well, it's been good seeing you again, Rogan. Guess I'd better get back to the party now." Her high heels sank into the plush rose-colored Aubusson carpet with every step she took.

She'd known the chances of getting out of the room unscathed were somewhere between poor and dismal. Still, it had been worth a try.

He snared her arm in a gentle vise. His nails were immaculately manicured, his fingers long and lean with just a slight roughness of dark hair on the back of his hand. The watch he wore was worth a month of her pay. His musky male scent spoke with equal eloquence of his wealth, as did the tux that emphasized the contours of his well-developed physique— broad shoulders, lean hips and long, long legs. Even though she wore three-inch heels, she had to look up to Rogan. And she'd certainly never been considered petite.

"Maybe before you leave you ought to tell me why you were going through Geoffrey's safe."

"Is that what I was doing?" Sam rued the fact that stubby red eyelashes—even with three coats of mascara—didn't bat worth a darn, innocent or not.

"There has been a rash of jewel thefts around L.A. lately. I don't suppose your visit to Geoffrey's study and opening his safe has anything to do with that."

"Perhaps I should ask what brought *you* upstairs when obviously the party is still in full swing. Maybe you had some special interest in Geoffrey's study yourself?"

"I'm hiding out from a woman from Florida who's got marriage on her mind."

"I see." Sam's stomach tensed unnecessarily. His romantic interludes were none of her business. The fact that her childhood fantasies about Rogan continued to reappear periodically was purely coincidental. "Still playing the field, are you?"

"Absolutely." He eyed her with renewed appreciation. "When I find someone interesting to play with."

That damn blush swept over her again. Somebody ought to invent a pill…

The study door burst open.

"There you are, Rogan!" Geoffrey strode into the room breathlessly. His lank blond hair looked tousled and his face glistened with perspiration as though he'd been dancing to the hard-rock beat downstairs. When he spotted Sam, he smiled slyly and gave her a wink. "Ah, I should have known Rogan would find our Samantha first thing. Smashing, I'd say. Getting acquainted, are we?"

"Actually, we've known each other for some time," Rogan responded.

Sam winced. He was going to blow her cover big-time. So much for career progression.

"Then you must know the Boston Sterlings. Samantha's one of them. Old money, I understand. Top drawer." Geoffrey's British accent made the *a* in drawer sound like a whole syllable unto itself.

"I know her family." Rogan looped his arm around her shoulder and gave Sam a squeeze. It was not necessarily a gesture of affection. More like a warning to shut up, which she should have been asking him to do if she was going to keep her past a secret.

But Sam did as she was told. What the hell was Rogan's scheme, anyway? Or was he simply covering his own tracks? Successful jewel thieves were not, by definition, stupid. And he didn't have a much better excuse for being in Geoffrey's study than she did. There were diamonds in that safe. Maybe emeralds, too. She felt it in her gut.

In spite of her better judgment, she hated the

thought that Rogan might be the thief. But she was a professional and emotion couldn't play a part in her actions. He was on a short list of fifteen possible suspects. So was Geoffrey. Somewhere there was a stash of diamonds and emeralds. She intended to find them.

"Seems to me you promised me a dance, Sam." Taking her elbow with a firm grip, Rogan eased her past Geoffrey toward the door of the study. "Come on, Carrot Top."

Picking up her clutch purse from the desktop and tucking it under her arm, Sam seethed. Rogan knew she hated that nickname. He'd pinned it on her when she'd been only eight years old, the daughter of the Prescott's new live-in housekeeper. He'd been the spoiled younger son of the family—eight years her senior—with more time on his hands than good sense. By the time she was thirteen and her mother had taken a better paying job elsewhere, Sam had been hopelessly, helplessly in love with Rogan, or so it had seemed from her adolescent perspective as she recalled the devastatingly handsome Harvard man he'd become. Not that he'd done anything more than give her grief.

Maybe she should hope she could return the favor.

ROGAN WOULD NEVER have expected Sam to come to this. A safecracker? A thief?

She'd been full of spunk as a kid, he admitted. A tomboy through and through. But a criminal? That was hard to swallow. Even the thought left the bitter taste of disappointment at the back of his throat.

The Prescott family had always made it a point to take care of their servants, a paternalistic attitude, no doubt. Even if he had caught Sam red-handed, he wouldn't want to turn her over to the police. She'd almost been like a little sister to him.

He ran his thumb across the warm, velvety skin of her inner elbow and felt a fine shudder ripple through her. Hell, it was too bad he had such brotherly feelings toward her. Especially since she filled out that slinky dress to perfection.

As they reached the bottom step of the curving staircase, the music began to throb again. The hardwood floors vibrated with it and the crystal chandelier quivered to the rhythm.

"Why don't we go outside where we can talk," he suggested, still gripping her elbow.

"If you don't mind, I'll, uh..." She glanced around. "I think I'll find the ladies' room and—uh—freshen up."

"I'll go with you."

"Thanks, anyway. I can manage on my own."

He cocked an eyebrow. "Too bad. I'd love to help. But mostly I don't want you to do an imitation of a rabbit before we've gotten a chance to get reacquainted."

She glared at him, her perfectly arched eyebrows lowering. Her eyes were a deep shade of green, or maybe they were reflecting the color of her dress. Either way, it was a dynamite combination.

They both knew she planned to slip out a back door and do a vanishing act once she was out of sight. Rogan didn't intend to let that happen.

She pressed out a sigh that sounded anything but defeated. "What do you want from me, Rogan?"

Several images came to mind, most of them centering around a week spent together on his yacht sailing through the tropics. A *leisurely* week. Maybe longer. And then he remembered they were practically relatives. "For now, conversation will do."

"Yoo-hoo! Rogan, dear!"

He stifled a groan. However much he loved his great-aunt Agatha, this was not the time he wanted to talk to her.

She swept up to him, her gown right out of the twenties, beads and fringe swaying, her fingers loaded with expensive-enough rings for a down payment on the biggest house in Bel Air.

She kissed him on the cheek. "How is my favorite nephew this evening? Wonderful party, isn't it? I do believe I've danced every dance, though some of these young fellows do have an endurance problem. They simply can't keep up." She finally took a breath and gave Sam an appreciative smile. "I see you've found the prettiest girl at the ball, Rogan. Just like you."

There was no possible way he could get out of making an introduction. His aunt had probably spotted him with a pretty woman and couldn't contain her matchmaking curiosity. So he played along.

"Aunt Agatha, this is Samantha Sterling." He cleared the approaching lie from his throat. "Of the Boston Sterlings. Agatha Prescott." Thank goodness his aunt didn't seem to recognize Sam or he wouldn't have gotten away with the small, face-saving fib.

"Mrs. Prescott." Sam nodded, extending her hand.

"Oh, how lovely," Agatha gushed, taking Sam's offered hand between both of hers. "But do call me Aunt Agatha. Or just Agatha. Everyone does. You're here on holiday? You really must come for one of my brunches while you're in town. Rogan will bring you, won't you, dear boy? Where are you staying?''

''I, uh, met Geoffrey at the Beverly Hills Hotel. At the Polo Lounge.''

''A perfect selection, my dear. You must look absolutely stunning standing next to that pink stucco with your lovely red hair.''

''Aunt Agatha, I'm sure Sam didn't pick out the Beverly because it matched her hair.'' Assuming she was actually staying in that swanky, overpriced hotel, he thought. But maybe jewel thieves did just that, eager to mingle with those who had plenty of money.

''It's as good a reason as any to pick a hotel, don't you think?'' Agatha said with her usual distorted logic. ''Of course, if we all did that I'd have to stay at dreary gray hotels, wouldn't I? And I much prefer something more lively, as you well know.''

His aunt's infectious laughter made Rogan smile in spite of himself.

Sam responded with a soft echoing laugh that made him think of roasting hot dogs over an open fire at the beach and cuddling with her under a blanket as the summer evening turned cool. Her warmth struck him as unpretentious, very feminine and naturally appealing, in contrast to the women he knew who struggled to achieve the same illusion through guile.

With surprising difficulty, he set both the feeling and the intriguing image aside.

''Tell me, dear,'' unstoppable Agatha continued, ''I couldn't help but notice your earrings. Charming. Just charming. Are they real?''

''Yes, ma'am...Agatha.'' Fingering a dangling earring, Sam glanced at Rogan. *Guiltily,* he thought. "I prefer wearing real gems over imitations."

She wasn't exactly a good liar, he thought. Her cheeks took on a high color and she had trouble meeting his eyes. She'd probably stolen the damn things. Hell, he could have bought her that pair of earrings with the petty cash he had lying around the house.

"Do be careful with them, dear," Agatha admonished. "Just last week Marjorie Waller had a necklace stolen. Terrible thing. Of course, she's never been my favorite person. So parsimonious, you know. When I asked her to contribute a few pennies to Chandler House, she said no. Absolutely refused me." She shook her head. "Dreadful woman. And those emeralds looked too gaudy on her anyway."

"Maybe she gives to other charities," Rogan suggested.

"I doubt that. Some people simply lack a social conscience." She patted Rogan on the cheek. "Sweet boy. Well, I'm off, then. My dancing partners have probably recovered their wind by now." Turning to Sam, she said, "Do have Rogan bring you by, my dear. We'll talk all about Boston and I'll tell you about Chandler House. Wonderful organization, you know. So important. The emeralds would have looked much nicer on you, my dear, but of course they're gone now." With that, she swept away toward the room where the band was playing, the fringe on her dress shimmering.

In unison, Sam and Rogan exhaled.

"Amazing," Sam said, smiling after the departing figure. Just listening to Aunt Agatha had worn her out. She didn't think she'd ever had that much energy and didn't expect to have it at Agatha's age.

"She's eighty-six and can run rings around me and everyone else I know." Rogan glanced over his shoulder. "Come on, let's get something to eat."

"I really should be going." If she could find a way, Sam wanted to slip back upstairs and revisit that safe. But she'd have to ditch Rogan first.

When he cupped her elbow again, she knew that wasn't going to be easy. *Determined man.*

The buffet table was weighted with dozens of different dishes including molded caviar, hot lobster bits in a cream sauce, chicken divan and more salads than Sam could count. She remembered helping her mother serve meals like this, with the assistance of an army of caterers. It was darn hard work and she smiled at the man slicing the turkey and prime rib, uncomfortable that she was on this side of the serving table under false pretenses.

"Just a sliver, on the rare side, if you have it," she requested, tamping down the inner voice that told her not to get too used to the role she was playing. She'd never really *belong* mixing with the rich and famous.

The server deftly carved a slice and slid it on to her plate, pouring a little juice over the top when she nodded her approval. Like most well-trained servants, he was anonymous in appearance. Any man wearing a white jacket and chef's hat would look the same, making him almost unidentifiable unless you were taking particular note. Or had some special training.

Sam did.

She'd already spotted a small spidery tattoo in the web between his thumb and first finger on the right hand. His eyes were a nondescript shade of hazel, but they protruded slightly. He was nearly a perfect character to move unnoticed through any crowd—the kind who could lift a wallet so smoothly the victim wouldn't even be aware it was gone.

Or maybe she was just suspicious of everyone these days.

Rogan Prescott included.

She caught the eye of a waiter dressed in a dark dinner jacket. A tall, slender man, his ginger-blond hair was slicked down a little too carefully. When he came in her direction, she lifted a flute of champagne from the tray he carried.

"I trust everything is satisfactory, miss."

"Not entirely," she said under her breath.

"My employer will be sorry to hear that."

"Tell me about it," she grimaced.

Rogan came up behind her. "I've found us a place to sit in the library."

"Wonderful." Sighing, she gave the waiter a departing shrug.

"Can't stop fraternizing with the help?" Rogan asked as he expertly juggled his plate and glass while pulling out a chair for her at a felt-covered game table.

She took his remark as a reminder that she'd been raised to use the backstairs along with the rest of the servants. "It never hurts to be friendly," she said coolly.

"Or maybe that young, good-looking stud is your partner."

Her fork—sterling silver with a traditional swirling

pattern—stopped midway to her mouth. How had he guessed that? "My partner?"

"I imagine a good safecracker would have a partner he—or she—could pass the goods off to in order to get away clean."

Relaxing, she ate the bite of lobster that had been halted midair. The flavor was extraordinarily delicate. If she'd been in the market for a caterer, she certainly would have checked with Geoffrey to get the name of whoever was serving this party.

Unfortunately, for the infrequent parties she threw her budget could only handle Chinese take-out, or pizza and beer. Her tastes, however, had no such limitation.

She savored a piece of prime rib. Superb. The horseradish had just the right amount of zest.

"So are you ready to tell me why you were rummaging through Geoff's safe?" Rogan asked. He broke a roll in two and spread butter on it. The front view of Sam was fully as pleasant as the rear view had been. Impertinent breasts challenged the silk fabric to a duel of strength. His aunt had been right. An emerald necklace, a single stone that nestled right above the cleavage, would be a perfect accessory for Sam. With matching earrings, of course.

"How do you know I didn't find it standing open?"

"Did you?"

Rather than answering his question, she feigned interest in spearing a marinated string bean that kept sliding across her plate. Breaking into safes was a special talent she'd picked up from a boy in high school whose father had been a locksmith.

"So how did you wrangle an invitation to this little soiree?" he asked as an alternative question.

She glanced up. "If you must know, I met Geoffrey at a luncheon he was hosting at the Beverly Hills Hotel. Something about his import business. He was kind enough to invite me tonight."

"About the only thing he imports is a lot of hot air."

"Oh? From the looks of his house, he seems to be quite successful."

Rogan had wondered about that, too. He figured the house was leased but it still required a lot of pounds sterling to keep a place this size afloat. The Pacific Palisades was a pricey location. And Geoffrey had no visible means of support, though he billed himself as a big-time wheeler-dealer.

Choosing not to say his thoughts aloud, Rogan asked, "Are you really staying at the Beverly Hills Hotel?"

"Why would I lie about a thing like that?"

"You wouldn't. Unless you have something to hide."

Her gaze slid away from his. "Geoffrey made that assumption when I met him. I didn't see any reason to tell him different."

"So where do you live?"

"You're being pushy, Rogan. Maybe I'd just as soon you not know where I live."

Absently, he ate a bite of lobster. Steak was more to his liking—thick, juicy and rare. "Maybe I'd like to give you a call one of these days."

Her eyes snapped back to meet his. Frosty green

daggers sailed across the table at him. "Don't bother. I have an unlisted number."

Rogan chuckled. He'd always enjoyed raising Sam's hackles, particularly since, even as a kid, she'd been able to hold her own. Now that she was all grown up, it was even more fun. Every man needed a little sister to tease.

"So besides knocking off safes now and then, what have you been up to all these years?"

"This and that," she parried. "How about you? Did you join the family business?"

"Not a chance. I've left that pleasure entirely to my brother." He tasted the prime rib. Not bad. "You married?"

"No. You?"

He shook his head. What an evasive little devil she was. But he loved just looking at her, contemplating the swell of her breasts and the quick flash of a reluctant smile as she sparred with him. Sam Sterling had definitely not grown into a wimpy woman. He liked that—a lot.

As he was taking another bite, enjoying every moment of his conversation with Sam, a set of decidedly female fingernails skimmed along the back of his neck. Startled, he looked up.

"Hello, sweet'ums." Marijoe Putney smiled down at him, her doe-eyed gaze darting to Sam and back again. "Haven't seen you in a coon's age," she drawled, her phony South Carolina accent gaining thickness with every word.

"Must be because there aren't that many coons around L.A.," he suggested. He gave her a quick smile, then turned back to Sam, hoping Marijoe would get the message.

The message in Sam's eyes was filled with cool disapproval. Hell, he couldn't help it if a woman stopped by to say hello.

"A friend of yours?" Sam asked icily after Marijoe had walked away.

"An acquaintance. That's all."

"The lady from Florida who you were hiding from?"

"Nah. She's South Carolina. Florida's a blonde. She's probably found someone else by now." He hoped.

Sam's smile looked a little strained. "I'd be happy to vacate the premises if you'd rather have dinner with either of them."

His lips quirked. "Not a chance, *sweet'ums.* I'm having too much fun sparring with you."

She gave him a dirty look and it was all he could do not to laugh out loud. Samantha Sterling was proving to be one of the most challenging women he'd ever met—a top-notch candidate for Sister of the Year...if she hadn't been a thief.

Not that his thoughts didn't have a tendency to drift into an area that wasn't at all brotherly. Damn, he was going to have to watch himself.

ALMOST THE INSTANT they had cleaned their plates, that good-looking waiter showed up to take them away. He did it smoothly, professionally. A little too much so, in Rogan's view.

"The desserts have been set out, sir, when you and the lady are ready. Or I'd be happy to bring you coffee, if you'd like, sir." The guy's voice dripped with deference that didn't quite ring true.

Rogan didn't like the waiter. He looked like a guy who would smile the whole time he was picking your pocket. "Later," he mumbled, sending the guy into a vanishing act.

"I'm really not joking this time." Graceful as a ballet dancer, Sam stood. She smiled down at Rogan with full, kissable lips. For an instant Rogan imagined heaven. "I've got to find the ladies' room."

"Sure. Go ahead." With his protective instincts on full alert—plus a full load of suspicions—Rogan watched her wander off in the same direction the waiter had gone. He wasn't pleased. She deserved better.

He waited about thirty seconds, then followed them. He'd reached a long, empty hallway that led to the back of the house when he heard a woman scream.

"My necklace! Someone's stolen my necklace!"

Rogan cursed. Damn, she was quick! Or that waiter was.

In a few long strides, he went the length of the hallway. He turned the corner and there was Sam, *pretending* to be going in the door to the john when he guessed she'd already been inside, maybe hiding the loot.

He grabbed her hand. "Come on, sweetheart. I know a way out the back."

"What are you doing?" she protested. "I've gotta go!"

"I'm saving your hide, that's what." He tugged her

into a family parlor room. "This place is going to be swarming with cops any minute."

"Have you gone out of your mind? You're going to yank my arm out of its socket."

"The lady you or your partner nabbed the necklace from has already blown the whistle. The smart thing to do is to get out of here."

"Rogan! Stop!"

He did. Right outside the back door when he met a uniformed rent-a-cop coming up the porch steps. The gun on his hip was an instant argument stopper.

"I'm sorry, sir. Miss. I'll have to ask you both to step back into the house."

"Of course, Officer." Reversing direction, Rogan tucked his arm through Sam's. "Remember, you don't have to say a word," he said under his breath. "If they arrest you, they won't set the bail very high. I'll hire an attorney for you first thing in the morning. You'll be out in no time."

"That's very generous of you, Rogan, but I doubt that will be necessary."

"If I have a chance, I'll tell them you were with me when the necklace was stolen."

"But I wasn't, Rogan. As far as I know, *you* could have lifted the necklace."

"Me?" he sputtered. "You've got to be kidding. Where's your sense of loyalty?"

"*I'm* supposed to be loyal to you?"

"Yeah, why not?"

"You gave me nothing but grief when I was growing up."

He frowned. All he'd ever done was tease her a little. She'd been so darn gullible. And that's what a surrogate brother was supposed to do. "It was good for you. Made you strong."

"It gave me a pain in the butt."

Moving them along, the rent-a-cop ushered them into the room where the couples had been dancing. The band was quiet now; the woman who'd been robbed, hysterical. Rogan knew her. Monica Lankershim was the sole support of a dozen Beverly Hills plastic surgeons. She tried to pass herself off as a wealthy widow of under forty. The masquerade wasn't very successful, though she found plenty of men to share her bed on a temporary basis—including his brother Adam, he suspected.

As upset as Monica might be, Rogan had trouble generating a great deal of sympathy for her. She was a phony and a user. He didn't like either of those attributes.

The rent-a-cops, plus the real thing when they arrived, tried to sort through all the chaos. Couples were separated for questioning, while Aunt Agatha roamed unmolested through the crowd trying to calm the excited women.

When Rogan looked around, he saw Sam being led off by one of the blue uniforms. She looked grim.

"Ah, hell," he muttered. He hoped she'd had enough sense to stash the necklace or to pass it off to her partner, if she'd been the one to snatch it. At least she ought to know enough to keep her mouth shut.

The recent rash of jewel thefts in town had gotten a lot of influential people up in arms, including the mayor. It wasn't all that hard to imagine a lynch mob forming to go after the culprit. Most of these socialite women spent hours on the tennis court every week, and quite a few worked out on a regular basis at a gym. They were a tough bunch, not one he'd want to cross.

Rogan didn't want Sam to be the first victim of their vigilantism.

## Chapter Two

The September sun had already heated the streets of West Los Angeles when Sam arrived at the police station. Sweat tracked down between her breasts as she went inside. Anxiety purled along her spine.

She flashed her ID in the direction of the security personnel at the entrance. He waved her through and she took the stairway to the detective division.

For a rookie cop on her first undercover assignment, she'd certainly ended up in the middle of a fiasco last night. There would be hell to pay with her supervisor.

In contrast to last evening, Sam was wearing slacks and a suit jacket that hid her shoulder holster. She'd gratefully slid her tired feet into sensible shoes this morning. Three-inch heels had obviously been designed by a sadistic male. Her toes still felt pinched and her calves might never recover from the ordeal.

Entering the office, she knew she'd been right. She was in trouble. Bobby Jackson, her temporary partner and last night's waiter, didn't even glance in her direction. She could almost hear the funeral march playing—or hear the orders being typed that would send her back to patrol. She'd only been out of the academy four weeks. When they'd pulled her off patrol for this undercover assignment, she'd thought it was her lucky break. After the mess last night, she wasn't so sure.

Detective Luis Garcia, his face creased at least once for every arrest he'd made in his twenty-some years on the force, crooked his finger at her. They said Garcia was a top cop. That didn't necessarily make him easy to like.

Straightening her shoulders, she crossed the room, gave Bobby a smile when he finally acknowledged her presence, and nodded to her supervisor. "Good morning, Detective. Beautiful day, isn't it?"

He didn't return her greeting. Instead, he crossed his arms and gave her one of those scowls meant to intimidate the most hardened felon. It was pretty darn effective even with Sam—but she wasn't about to back off. She'd wanted to be a cop since her senior year in high school. She'd worked hard to even get on the force. And if she'd had some doubts during the past few weeks of actually being on the job, she was still determined to be the best darn cop the L.A.P.D. had ever seen. Once she made up her mind, she didn't do things halfway. And her two friends who had died so innocently while standing right next to her deserved to have their memories honored with the best effort she could make.

"Now listen up, *Officer* Sterling." Garcia said her title with a sneer. "Would you care to explain how a ten-thousand-dollar necklace vanished while you and your partner were practically standing guard over it?"

Sam forcefully set aside the sudden onslaught of

memories that threatened to overwhelm her. Marcia and Dee wouldn't be well served if she let Garcia see just how vulnerable she was. "I don't know, sir."

"So what did you find out about Geoffrey Hughes?"

"Except for learning there is a jewelry box in his safe, I'm afraid not much. My investigation was interrupted."

"We had a special warrant for that search, Sterling. I didn't expect you to blow it."

"I'm sorry, sir."

Jackson cleared his throat. "Rogan Prescott, one of our prime suspects, distracted her, sir."

She shot Bobby a startled look. Her partner didn't have to say it quite like that. He could have made it sound as if she'd been engaged in good police work. Which, of course, she hadn't been. She'd been careless.

Careless with a millionaire playboy who had women falling all over themselves trying to attract his attention. As far as Sam was concerned, that made a man poison—and in Rogan's case, maybe a thief, as well. Certainly a thief of hearts.

Besides, *distraction* was an understatement when it came to describing Rogan. Though that had certainly happened after she'd been caught with her fingers in the safe.

Moving purposefully into her personal space, Detective Garcia glowered at her. He'd had *huevos rancheros* with onions for breakfast. Lots of onions. "Is that so? One of our suspects?"

She stood her ground. "Mr. Prescott came into the library while I was searching the safe."

"He caught you?"

"Yes, sir."

Garcia swore. "What did he do?"

"He escorted her to supper," Jackson told the detective.

"I knew the man, sir," she snapped. "From a long time ago. I *had* to go with him or he would have blown my cover."

One corner of Detective Garcia's lips hitched into a weak imitation of a smile. "He caught you with your hand in the cookie jar and he didn't blow the whistle? You musta known him pretty well."

"I don't think he wanted me to get in trouble. I think..." In spite of herself, Sam licked her lips self-consciously. "He thinks *I'm* the jewel thief we've been looking for."

With glacial slowness, as though his facial muscles were unfamiliar with the task—or he'd just thought of the most wonderful joke in the world—the detective's face shifted into a full-blown smile and he laughed. The rough, rusty sound boomed through the room and the few detectives hanging around on a Saturday morning turned to stare.

"I'll be damned! If he's our culprit, he probably thinks you're the competition. That's great!"

Easy for him to say. Rogan had almost blown her cover in his eagerness to drag her out the back way, not that there hadn't been plenty of other women at the party who would have been happy to have him drag them out the back door. As it was, she'd had to do some mighty fast talking with the patrol officers to avoid being questioned with the other party-goers.

Garcia rubbed his hands together almost gleefully.

"Now then, Jackson, what did you get on the servants and caterers?"

"Not much, sir. A couple of the catering people are on our list of possibles because they were on the scene of prior thefts. But they were both pretty close-mouthed about the whole thing."

Sam recalled the man who had been serving the turkey and prime rib and wondered if he was on the list. He'd had quick hands. She'd have to check with Jackson later.

"We're getting a lot of pressure from upstairs on this thing, people," Garcia said. "We're going to have to knuckle down and make ourselves a break. Jackson, I want you to work every party you can. Become one of 'em with the catering folks. Go out afterward and drink beer with 'em. Whatever it takes. Servants always know more than they let on."

"Yes, sir." With obvious relief for not having had his head handed to him, Jackson settled one hip on the edge of a cluttered desk. His hair wasn't slicked back this morning and it hung limply from a part in the middle.

The lead detective returned his attention to Sam, his imitation of a smile now little more than a smirk. "Listen up, young lady, I want you to *cozy* up to this Prescott character."

"Cozy up?" She didn't like the sound of that. Nor did she appreciate his condescending attitude, but she'd long since learned that went with the territory for a woman on the force. Affirmative action didn't always mean a whole lot down in the trenches.

"Yeah. Like Jackson, I want you to be practically in his pants."

That particular metaphor held little appeal. At least, she hoped her supervisor meant it only as a manner of speaking. Among other things, she suspected Rogan's pants were a prime target for a good many other women, and hated that after all these years that thought would bother her so much. She certainly had no claim on him now any more than she'd had as a thirteen-year-old, however much she used to dream it would be so. "Sir, I really don't think—"

"What? You're on loan, Sterling. A rookie. You don't *think*. You take orders, got that, sweetheart? We put together that cover story for you to hang around that pink hoity-toity hotel, and got you that fancy wardrobe."

"From a consignment store," she commented.

"It's your *job* to play the part of a wealthy broad on the make. Or a thief, if that's what he thinks. Prescott's a cool character and that's damn suspicious to me, particularly since he shows up on our lists of attendees at a lot of the crime scenes."

"So does Geoffrey Hughes."

"Yeah? You wanna get into Hughes's pants, too? It's okay by me, if you can handle two guys at once."

Sam gritted her teeth. She'd love to bring Garcia up on harassment charges but it wouldn't do her career any good. Unless things got totally out of hand, a woman was supposed to have a thick skin. "No, sir, that's not what I meant."

"You're not shy, are you, *Officer* Sterling?"

Damn right she was, when it came to spending time with Rogan Prescott. "I simply think it would be inappropriate for me to contact him directly. He'd become suspicious."

"Then see to it you just happen to be the same places he is." Garcia cocked a suggestive brow. "He'll get the message that you're available."

She fought the heated flush that threatened to creep up her neck. She was *not* "available" to Rogan—and never would be. She had no interest in a man who had an entourage of females tagging along after him, most of whom, she assumed, probably suffered from a broken heart.

But it did appear that if she wanted to keep her job and have decent performance reviews, she would have to deal with him. Taking an optimistic view, she decided spending time with Rogan Prescott would be the perfect antidote for her lingering adolescent crush on the man.

"He said something about trying to call me," she admitted reluctantly. "But I've got an unlisted number."

"So we'll get it listed."

She sighed. Detective Garcia seemed to have an answer for everything. His evaluation of her work would make or break her career. She'd have to go along. Her career was that important to her—the payback for the deaths of her friends.

ROGAN TOOK A SWING at the golf ball and sliced it to the side of the fairway. It rolled into the rough, coming to a stop only inches away from the trunk of a giant pine tree.

"Tough luck," Adam said.

Shrugging, Rogan picked up his tee. About once a month Rogan and his brother got together for a round of golf. Adam, who used golf like a corporate tool, kept his game as sharp as his negotiating skills. Through the years he'd made a lot of successful deals over the course of eighteen holes. It had worked for their father, and Adam had inherited the knack.

Rogan preferred volleyball on the beach, which gave him a hefty handicap on the golf course.

"Thought I'd see you at Geoff's shindig last night," Rogan said. He climbed into the passenger seat of the golf cart and Adam accelerated down the asphalt path toward their balls.

"I was otherwise occupied," Adam replied. "Pleasantly occupied."

"Oh? What's her name?"

Adam slanted Rogan a glance filled with locker room machismo. "I don't think you've met her."

Although five years separated them in age, physically they were about the same size and both had the Prescott smile. But Adam had a streak of alley cat in him that Rogan had trouble accepting. Not that he had a right to throw stones in his brother's direction. Rogan had never been involved in a relationship that lasted more than a few months, but he hadn't compounded the problem by getting married. He figured he'd inherited the Prescott gene that made commitment impossible.

He recalled a college experience when he'd been dating a perfectly nice girl, a girl any reasonable guy would have latched on to permanently. But it simply didn't work for Rogan. Finally, he'd called it off. According to her friends, she'd been so devastated she'd switched schools and eventually dropped out. He didn't think she ever graduated. And it was his fault because Prescotts had the power to mess up a woman's life even when, as in his case, they didn't intend to.

He always tried to keep that lesson in mind.

His brother didn't seem to care.

"You're not exactly being fair to Eileen, are you, Adam? She's always tried to be a decent wife to you." As far as Rogan could tell, Adam didn't treat his mistresses much better than his wife. He considered all women disposable when they no longer suited his taste.

"Don't lecture me, little brother. Remember, I'm the one who runs the family business and makes all those nice dividends for you every quarter."

"The prospect of making rows and rows of sparkling porcelain toilets and selling them at inflated prices has never thrilled me."

"But you're willing enough to spend the profits. Besides, if I feel the need for a little relaxation, it's only because I deserve it." He slid Rogan a sly, arrogant smile. "After all, I'm the original ladies' man, aren't I?"

"Just like dear ol' dad, right?"

Adam halted the cart near Rogan's ball. "I never heard our mother complain, at least not when she decked herself out in all the finery he bought her and drove around in a new Mercedes convertible every year. She got what she wanted by marrying Dad."

"Maybe." But Rogan had seen her cry once. He'd been about six, but he'd never forgotten that heartbreaking sound. He'd vowed he wouldn't bring that kind of grief upon any woman. As far as he could tell, marrying a Prescott was hell for a woman.

"Eileen isn't one of your charity cases," Adam

reminded him. "And she's not a stray you have to save, like you do with every Tom, Dick and Harry beach bum who shows up at your door. She's doing just fine. I give her exactly what she needs."

Without responding, because the thought of Eileen suffering the same hurt their mother had experienced was too unpleasant to deal with, Rogan swung out of the cart and pulled a two wood from his bag. "Might as well give me a penalty shot on this hole. No way am I going to try to shoot out from behind that tree."

"Okay. But remember, you're going to owe me a hundred dollars a point."

"I've got my checkbook with me. As usual." Rogan guessed his losses on the golf course would buy Adam's current mistress a trinket or two. Or maybe Eileen. He didn't know whether he should feel guilty about that or not.

Strangely, he had the odd notion Sam could tell him the ethical thing to do. He'd been thinking about her a lot since he'd seen her being led off by the police last night. He'd even called one of his buddies on the L.A.P.D. this morning to see if she'd actually been arrested. There'd been no record. Apparently she'd talked her way out of trouble. This time.

As he dropped the ball over his shoulder, he wondered how she could have gone so far wrong. A jewel thief!

Maybe when he finished his round with Adam, he'd use a couple of his connections to get hold of that unlisted number of hers. Just to see if she was okay. He might even see if they could get together sometime. Aunt Agatha was hosting one of her fund-raising parties tonight.

Sam was young enough that she could still turn her life around. *If* she had some help. And a concerned big brother to look after her.

TWO PARTIES in two days. Sam hadn't had a social life like this since her college years. And then she'd inevitably been sorry.

When she spotted Rogan across the width of the hotel ballroom filled with banquet tables, she thought she'd probably regret it this time, too.

Even from a distance, his smile was an invitation to trouble. Lord, how she remembered him flashing her that devil-may-care grin when she was a kid. It hadn't meant anything then and it didn't now, she reminded herself. But it still made her heart tap-dance in her chest.

If Detective Garcia hadn't ordered her to get into Rogan's pants—figuratively, she hoped—she never would have accepted his phone call, much less agreed to join him at this charity event.

She made a quick sweep of the crowd, trying to pick out Bobby Jackson. She didn't see him but she did spot the guy with the protruding eyes and spidery tattoo from the prior evening. He was carrying a tray of drinks. She'd have to keep her eye on him.

"I was afraid you might change your mind."

Sam jumped at the sound of Rogan's voice so close to her. Her startled reaction no doubt accounted for the strange fluttery sensation in her stomach that went along with the rapid beat of her heart.

She forced a smile and looked up at him. Damn, he had gorgeous eyes, so bright a blue they looked like polished agates. They absolutely sparkled with mischief. The lock of walnut-brown hair that had slipped over his forehead would tempt any woman to touch.

"How could I have possibly refused your gracious, last-minute invitation?" she asked innocently. *Particularly when my boss made it abundantly clear my performance review depended upon my getting close to you. Very close.*

"I didn't know until last night that you'd grown up into a 'ten,' Carrot Top." His lips canted into a wry grin and that magical dimple appeared.

She blinked, trying to decide whether she ought to react first to his stupid nickname for her or his rating of her. With a flippant toss of her head that sent her curls dancing, she decided on the latter. "A 'ten'? You flatter me. I've never thought of myself as more than a nine-and-a-half."

He lightly tapped the tip of her nose with his fingertip. "Don't underestimate yourself, Sam. Most of the guys in this room would give you an eleven, but I don't want you to get a swelled head."

A woman's legs should not go rubbery at a comment like that. Or at such a fleeting touch. So Sam locked her knees and stiffened her spine. She was not going to believe one single word this playboy said. Not one! Silver tongue be damned.

Never in her life had she been thought of as beautiful. She had far too many freckles. And her hair didn't even bear discussing. Not that she was ugly, of course. But she'd spent a lot of hours in front of the mirror as an adolescent coming to grips with how she really looked. *Unique* appeared to be the best description she could come up with, all things considered. She'd learned to live with that.

In contrast, every female she'd seen hanging around Rogan at the Prescott estate had been model perfect.

Slipping his arm around her waist, he said, "Come on. We're at table four. Right up front. The food ought to be great but I won't guarantee the speeches."

"What kind of a charity event *is* this?" she managed to ask, acutely aware of the warmth of his hand at her midriff and her still-unsettled reaction to his comment. A flashbulb went off somewhere nearby, but she hardly noticed. The heat on her face had far more to do with Rogan and how closely he held her.

"It's one of Aunt Agatha's pet charities. It's probably Chandler House, but it could just as well be Save the Dust Bunnies or Cure Ingrown Toenails. I forget which."

Laughing, she jabbed him in the ribs with her elbow. "You're terrible."

"Yeah," he drawled. "Ain't it grand?"

No, it wasn't. Sam didn't want to like Rogan. She didn't want him to be fun or to make her laugh. What if he really was the jewel thief? How would she ever be able to turn over evidence against him to her superiors? Much less testify in a court of law to put him behind bars?

Even the thought made her slightly sick to her stomach.

The situation wouldn't be much better if he was *not* a crook. She knew his family and the social set they traveled with a little too well. Fidelity in relationships was not high on their priority list. For Sam, it was right up on top..

In spite of her adolescent fantasies, Rogan Prescott was definitely not a man she would want to fall for. He would bring nothing but heartache. Just like her father, a man who had deserted his wife and child to be with another woman—and never looked back.

As if to confirm her thoughts, a young woman with glorious blond hair and a pixie face sidled up to Rogan. Without preamble, she kissed him on the cheek.

"You promised to call," she said sweetly. "I'm still waiting."

"I've got your number, dollface." Without hardly missing a beat, he returned the kiss, his hand still firmly cupping Sam's elbow.

Sam firmly tamped down a raging case of unwarranted jealousy. She didn't have any claim on Rogan—didn't want one, thank you very much. Her mother's experience had made it very clear that dreams could sometimes turn into nightmares.

A few moments later, as she and Rogan wove their way around the tables, Sam was struck by the sheer elegance of the other guests. Every man wore a tux, every woman wore jewels worth a king's ransom— necklaces and earrings, bracelets that dripped diamonds or glowed with gold. One rather daring soul had a nose ring sporting a diamond that had to be more than a karat. This party was a mecca for a prospective jewel thief, a temptation few criminals would be able to resist.

She touched the diamond earrings she wore. Detective Garcia would have her job—and her hide—if she lost them.

If Rogan was the thief, he'd picked the perfect place to ply his trade.

If he wasn't a crook, and still suspected *she* had sticky fingers, it was darn odd he'd bring her to a party like this.

Catching whiffs of perfume and aftershave as they passed through the crowd—some potent and others far more subtle—her senses instinctively sought out that distinctive scent she connected with Rogan. Masculine. Powerful without being overpowering. Blatantly sensual.

He greeted friends casually, his hand possessively at her waist, but didn't stop to introduce her. She bristled at the slight.

Thief or not, he'd invited her to this party. He ought to be willing to introduce her to his friends.

She experienced the same self-consciousness that she'd grown up with when the kids at Beverly Hills High looked down their respective noses at the housekeeper's daughter—until she'd helped to bring home a league championship trophy in girls' volleyball. Then she'd been their hero. That abrupt turnaround convinced Sam that what others thought of her didn't matter much.

She needed to remember that lesson this evening.

"There you are, dear girl!" Aunt Agatha burst out of a covey of society matrons standing near the speaker's podium. Her lacy hat had a brim two feet in diameter, making it look like she was wearing a pair of magenta wings. Or a hang glider. "I was so pleased when Rogan told me you were coming. I made him pay full price for the tickets, you know. It's such a good cause."

Agatha hooked an arm through Sam's. "Now I want you to take Rogan over to the silent auction table and get him to bid on whatever it is that takes your fancy. There's a trip to the Greek Isles that sounds lovely. Or a two-pound box of sinfully rich chocolates delivered to you every month for a year, if you'd like that."

"That probably wouldn't be good for my figure," Sam replied, feeling as though she was being swept along by a swirling tornado.

"Pshaw. A few extra calories wouldn't hurt you one whit. Would they, Rogan?"

"She looks fine to me just as she is."

"Here's your table, dear. Right next to mine. Let's just save these two seats so you won't have to turn around to hear the speaker. That's always such a bother. Put your purse here. No one will take it." Agatha whipped a fancily folded peach napkin from the goblet at the adjacent place and spread it over the setting to indicate the seat was taken. "I thought you and Rogan would want to sit with the younger crowd instead of with us old folks. Now be on your way to the silent auction before the festivities begin, and do make Rogan spend tons of money on you, dear. He has plenty, you know."

With that, Agatha scurried away to greet a distinguished looking gentleman and the beautiful blonde on his arm.

Reluctant to risk Agatha's ire, Sam placed her purse where she'd been instructed. She wasn't carrying much money—only cab fare home—so it would be no great loss if someone walked off with it. Her badge was a different matter. Detective Garcia would not be pleased if she lost that, nor would she.

Fortunately, her weapon—a 25-caliber Baretta—was tucked inside a neat little holster strapped to her thigh. Thanks to her flared skirt, no one would be the wiser unless she had to draw the thing in a hurry.

"Well, which will it be?" Rogan asked. "The Greek Isles or two inches around the waist?"

"Why don't we see if there are some other options."

Actually, there were dozens of prizes being auctioned off, all of them spread out on long tables against the far wall—exquisite baskets of silk flowers, a weekend on a forty-foot yacht, a year's lease for a new luxury car, and generous gift certificates from upscale shops on Rodeo Drive. Sam sensed Aunt Agatha had a hand in twisting every donor's arm. She was an amazing woman.

Among the crowd of bidders, Sam saw Geoffrey Hughes making his way up the line of displays. Several other faces looked familiar to her from last evening—including the doe-eyed woman who'd been so eager to greet Rogan last night. She waved across the width of the ballroom.

Rogan gave her a lazy wave in return.

"Do the same people go to all the same parties?" Sam asked him. It felt a little incestuous to her. When did they meet new people, or come in contact with new ideas? Or was the object simply to play hopscotch between an assortment of attractive bedmates, as she had suspected from the backstairs conversations she'd heard in the Prescott household when she'd been a child.

She watched as Rogan noted his bid on the sheet for the weekend yachting trip, three times as much as the previous offer...and several times more than its face value.

"Actually, I don't usually attend these things," he said as he set the clipboard aside. "I just send Agatha my contribution and she lets me off the hook as far as showing up is concerned."

"But you're here tonight?"

He casually picked up another bidding sheet. "Let's just say you inspired me."

Curious in spite of herself, she asked, "What is the tab for this evening's festivities?"

"I think Agatha said it was a thousand dollars a plate. To sit up front, anyway."

"A thou—" Sam choked and began coughing.

Rogan patted her on the back until she was able to pull herself together. "You all right? Can I get you a drink?"

"No, I'm fine." Her eyes watered and her throat was scratchy. "And I promise, at that price, I'll eat every single bite of my dinner. Even my vegetables."

"Don't forget dessert. It's included."

"I should hope so!" she sputtered, aghast at the way Rogan and his friends spent money with such ease. A ten-dollar early bird special was closer to her speed.

"Well, saving dust bunnies is important. We all have to pitch in and do our share." He laughed and hooked his arm around Sam's shoulders. He liked the way her eyes widened so expressively and how her full lips lifted into an unexpected smile at the darnedest things. He particularly liked the feel of her bare flesh, the pliant give of her smooth skin beneath his palm. It made it hard to remember he was supposed to be her surrogate brother.

She was wearing a spaghetti-strap dress tonight, one that he thought might be a Gucci design, though he couldn't be sure. However she was supporting herself, she was doing okay. But he hoped he was wrong about her being in the illicit business of snatching jewels. Given all the gems in the room, he'd have to keep a close eye on her.

Bringing her here had been the easy, natural thing to do. Until he got a good look at the rocks the other guests were wearing.

A drive-in movie on their own might have been smarter.

As the waiters began setting out the salads, Rogan led Sam back to the their table. Immediately the jovial man on Sam's left engaged her in conversation, to the exclusion of his meek little wife. With an effort, Rogan ignored the odd twist of jealousy that snaked through him so quickly he barely recognized it for what it was.

Most of the guests had found their places when Rogan heard a buzz of conversation start at the back of the room and then travel forward like a migrating swarm of bees. Glancing around, he spotted security people taking up positions by all the exits.

Damn! There'd been another robbery. He could feel it in his gut.

Surreptitiously, he opened Sam's clutch purse. Careful not to attract her attention, he shook the contents of the purse into his hand. A lipstick. Eyeliner. A slender wallet. A cell phone. And—

The glint of diamonds snaked into his palm, a pair of long, dangling earrings. Gaudy things, not to his taste—but worth a bundle.

He swore again. How had Sam moved so quickly that even *he* hadn't seen her lift them? But then, maybe he hadn't been watching her as carefully as he had thought.

Shoving the rest of the things back into her purse, he dropped the earrings into his jacket pocket and stood. He had to act fast before security tightened things down.

"I'll be right back," he said to Sam, flashing a smile across the table at the other guests who had joined them.

Frowning, Sam turned from the glorified used-car salesman who'd been monopolizing the conversation to watch Rogan walk away. Where could he be going in such a hurry when dinner was about to be served? The way he was making a beeline for the silent auction table, she wondered if he was going to raise his bid on something, bids that were already more than generous.

And then she noticed his hand slip into his jacket pocket as he reached the display. He pulled something out, and she saw a quick flash of reflected light as he dropped it under the table.

What on earth—

"Ladies and gentlemen, if I can have your attention, please." A burly man wearing a dark suit that didn't entirely disguise the bulge of his shoulder holster took command of the microphone on the podium. It didn't take a genius to realize he was not the programmed speaker, but hotel security.

"I want you all to remain calm and enjoy your meal," he continued. "However, one of our guests has misplaced her earrings and, while we're looking for them, we'd like for all of you to stay inside the ballroom. Thank you for your cooperation."

The decibel level in the room rose several notches as the news sank in with the audience.

Sam groaned. Rogan was the thief, all right. What he'd dropped under the table was a pair of earrings. She'd bet her L.A.P.D. badge on that. She could only guess that he'd spotted the security people and had decided to ditch the jewels so he wouldn't be caught. All things considered, that was a smart move.

Returning to their table, he slid into the seat beside her and rested his hand on her thigh. He came so close to touching her weapon, Sam nearly jumped out of her chair. His hand slid ever so slightly upward before coming to an abrupt halt. His eyes narrowed and a frown stitched across his forehead.

Damn, he'd either realized she was carrying a piece, or he was wondering what kind of peculiar garters she wore.

With an odd look in his eyes, he said, "I've taken care of everything, Sam. You don't have to worry."

"Me? Worry?" He was the one who was flirting with a ten-to-twenty-year sentence in Soledad State Prison for grand theft.

"They'll find the earrings in a few minutes. Everyone will think the woman simply dropped them, and then they'll get on with the party. No one will be the wiser."

"Rogan, you don't know what you're saying." She was a cop, and he had just confessed to having committed a major crime. Oh, man, she didn't want to be the one who sent him to jail.

"And when we get out of here, you're coming home with me."

"I'm what?" she gasped. "I can't go home with you."

The waiter delivered a dinner plate to the man on her left. As he leaned forward, she recognized Bobby Jackson. He whispered in her ear, "Listen up, Sam. You gotta do it. Garcia will give you a medal if you get the goods on this guy. And if you don't, he's likely to get you assigned to the file room until your retirement comes up."

Sam blanched. Jackson was probably right. But she couldn't go along with this kind of a proposition.

"Sorry, Rogan. I might have been the house-keeper's daughter, but that doesn't mean I want to play house with you."

He gave her a startled look. "Hey, that wasn't what I was talking about. Hell, you were practically my little sister. I wouldn't think of taking advantage of you."

He wouldn't? "Then why did you suggest—"

"Because I intend to reform you, Carrot Top." He squeezed her leg and a heated ribbon of sexual arousal that wasn't *at all* sisterly raced right up her thigh. "In my view, you are well worth saving."

He was going to reform *her?* He was the crook. Wasn't he?

"Rogan, I think you've been living in a rarefied atmosphere too long. I'm not exactly homeless, you know. I've got a place—"

Across the table, Bobby glared at her and mouthed the words, *"Do it."*

Sam glared back. Being a police officer didn't mean she had to go live with a guy, undercover or not.

"As I see it, you'd be a lot better off if you'd give up your current, uh…" Rogan hesitated a beat. "Occupation. You could find yourself some rich guy who'd buy you all the jewels you could want. You'd have a nice place to live. Fancy cars. And even if the marriage fell apart after a year or two, you'd still end up with a decent settlement that would keep you in diamonds for the rest of your life."

Maybe it was the noisy room, but Sam wasn't sure she was hearing right. "You're talking marriage?" To her?

"I've got a lot of connections, all of them in the right social and financial set. I figure with a little help from me, you could meet a guy and land him within a matter of months."

"You're talking about me marrying someone for his *money?*" Her voice cracked.

"Generally I don't approve of that, but under the circumstances I'd say it was better than—" he glanced around the table to be sure no one was listening "—stealing."

An irritated tic developed at the corner of her right eye. "That's very flattering." It was, in fact, the most insulting suggestion she'd ever heard.

"Great. Then when the party is over, we'll go to my place."

"Tonight? I didn't exactly bring a toothbrush with me."

"No problem. It will be late when this shindig is over. We can pick up your things tomorrow."

Bobby vigorously nodded his asinine approval, almost sliding the contents of the dinner plate he was serving into a guest's lap. If Sam didn't go along with Rogan's plan, she'd end up walking a beat. Or worse, stuck in a windowless office surrounded by musty files.

Dammit! She didn't want that! She wanted to prevent tragic deaths, and she couldn't do that sitting behind a desk.

"Tomorrow I'll start introducing you around," Rogan said. "And I'll give you some tips on how to act. You know, how to flatter a guy and make him feel like he's the most important person in the universe."

"You're going to tutor me in the fine art of landing a husband?" Worse and worse—Rogan's version of *My Fair Lady,* she gathered, deciding a bunch of violets would fit nicely down his craw.

He leaned back, his smile incredibly smug. "I bet that's the best offer you've ever gotten."

If there hadn't been an audience of five hundred present, she would have shown him just what she thought of his idea.

The nerve! The absolute gall of the man! To think she needed *his* help to land a husband!

But she did need his help to land a thief. And suddenly she didn't mind so much if she found out he was the culprit. The slamming of a steel door just might wipe that smug look off his face.

# Chapter Three

She'd made a serious mistake and now she was experiencing a severe case of cold feet.

She never should have agreed to go anywhere with Rogan. Certainly not home with him. She didn't want him to match her up with one of his wealthy buddies. She didn't even want to hang around with him!

What must he think of her?

As if she didn't know.

Sam juggled two huge silk flower arrangements in her arms and held the certificate Rogan had won for a weekend yachting trip between her teeth. Her purse was tucked under her arm.

"I'm surprised you live in Malibu," she said from between clenched teeth as she got out of his Bronco in front of a weathered gray structure. With these beachfront homes, there was barely enough space to park a car off the highway. All of them looked a little rundown. Somehow she'd expected him to live in a posh condo in Century City. Apparently she'd guessed wrong, just as she had been startled to discover he wasn't driving a Rolls-Royce or some equally luxurious car.

"Here, let me carry those." He tossed his tux jacket over his shoulder and relieved her of the floral baskets. "I guess you could say I'm a beach bum at heart."

As they approached the weathered-gray front gate, Sam's suspicious nature reared its ugly head like a rattlesnake about to strike. She simply couldn't take another step forward. No threat of a bad performance review or a return to patrol duty was worth this.

"Rogan, if this is some ploy for you to get me into the sack, it's not going to work."

He cocked his head. *"Moi?"* he asked innocently. "Why would you think that?"

"Because—" Because maybe that was what she secretly wanted. But she wasn't about to admit that, any more than she'd admit she'd seen his name on the invitation list that first evening and had, on some subconscious level, hoped—

"Don't give it another thought, Sam. You're as safe with me as a newborn lamb."

If that was the case, why did she have the feeling he was really a wolf in sheep's clothing? Either that or she'd totally overestimated her sex appeal, in which case she was mortally embarrassed.

Heat crept up her neck. Damn but she had a hard time reading Rogan. Even as a kid, she'd been slow to catch on when he'd been teasing her. Then she'd felt the fool.

Ten years hadn't changed things much.

Obviously she still couldn't hold a candle to all the model-perfect, society women he had at his beck and call.

"Come on in. I've got plenty of bedrooms. You can take your pick."

"I don't suppose it matters that I don't have anything to sleep in?"

He leaned on the gatepost, his lips quirked in an amused smile and his eyes narrowed. "I'll bet I can find you something."

Sam knew he had just mentally undressed her, however much he'd talked about this big brother business. She could all but feel the chilled sea air raising goose bumps on her heated flesh. His mixed signals were driving her crazy.

Without another word, he turned, walked through a tiny patio area with scruffy flower beds and went up the two steps to the front door.

Sam glanced around. Even at this late hour a steady stream of cars whizzed by on Pacific Coast Highway. She briefly considered hitchhiking home but thought better of it. Even calling a cab might not work in this remote location. And Garcia would be unlikely to come to her rescue.

She was stranded and could only hope Rogan wasn't a serial killer as well as a jewel thief. At least her fellow police officers would know where to look for her body if she didn't show up for a week or so. No doubt that's how long it would take them to miss her.

The instant Rogan opened the front door, a huge shaggy dog came bounding out. He woofed and leapt into the air, licking Rogan's face on the fly. His back end was wagging so hard, Sam thought sure he was going to break apart. Abandoning his master, he raced circles around Sam, sniffing and licking her hand, then finally rolling on the ground with his legs sticking straight up in the air. His tongue lolled to the side of his mouth as he panted.

In spite of herself, Sam laughed. She bent to scratch the dog's tummy. "If this creature is supposed to be a guard dog, you should ask for your money back."

"I'm afraid Goofus is a born comic. He might trample a burglar to death, but he'd never bite one."

"I don't think I'm familiar with this breed. What is he?"

"Beats me. My friend was going to breed her Lab but apparently before the pedigreed dog did his thing, somebody left a gate open. And voilá, along came Goofus. Cindy was so upset she was going to take the whole litter to the pound. But I figured I could handle at least one. Papers don't mean much to me. And a buddy who lives out in the desert took the other two."

"You rescued them?" From *Cindy?* A buxom blonde, no doubt.

Shrugging, Rogan stood holding the door open for her. "Come on, Carrot Top. Goofus doesn't bite and neither do I."

"That wasn't precisely what I was worried about," she mumbled. Warily, she edged past him. After his revelation about the dog, she was more concerned than ever she'd actually begin to *like* Rogan.

Toenails scrambling on the slate entryway, Goofus came slipping and sliding into the house right behind her. A throw rug pleated under his feet.

While the outside of the house might resemble a shanty, the inside was spectacular. The high ceilings, exquisite paintings on the walls, and the wide open view of the moonlit Pacific through wall-to-wall windows simply took Sam's breath away. The simple, almost rustic furnishings were placed so as not to detract from the grandeur of the sea.

Captivated, Sam strolled the length of the combined living and dining areas, her gaze both admiring and searching. It required considerable effort to remember she was a cop and was supposed to be looking for clues to a string of thefts—like wall safes where a crook might hide the loot. The oil paintings on display were each of unique style and exquisite, but she couldn't identify any of the painters. Not that she knew all that much about art.

As if Rogan had heard her unspoken question, he said, "They're all by Southern California artists. I'm a collector of sorts and I like to help out those with potential."

"You rescue starving artists, too?"

"I suppose I've been known to do that." He put the floral arrangements on the dining table. "One or two of the pieces I've bought ought to appreciate over time and become good investments. Meanwhile, I get to enjoy them."

She heard a touch of pride in his voice and wondered if it was the pleasure of identifying talent or the potential financial gain that pleased him the most. Or maybe just helping someone who needed his money.

Rogan Prescott increasingly appeared to be a more complex man than she had realized.

The phone rang. Rogan made no move to answer it, letting the machine on the breakfast bar pick up after the first ring.

Cocking an eyebrow, Sam listened to the caller in spite of knowing she shouldn't.

"Hi, sweet'ums. It's Marijoe," the voice drawled with sickening sweetness. "Sorry we didn't get to talk at the party. Call me, baby. I miss you." Her words were followed by a series of smacking noises Sam assumed were meant to be kisses. Then the machine clicked off.

Rogan appeared unmoved by the message. "She's a friend."

"Hope my being here won't cramp your style."

The corners of his eyes crinkled and he smiled. "I'll let you know if it's a problem."

Not sure whether to be amused or annoyed by the telephone incident, Sam allowed herself to be drawn to the back of the house. She noted a side room well furnished with exercise equipment but ignored it for the moment. The view of the ocean was simply irresistible.

Opening a sliding-glass door, she stepped outside onto a weathered deck. Waves hissed with a rhythmic splash against the narrow beach at low tide, drowning out any sounds from the highway. Salt-flavored air teased the back of her throat.

*Heaven,* she sighed.

She sensed rather than heard Rogan join her on the deck. Idly she wondered how many diamonds a person would have to steal before they could afford a place like this.

"The view is addictive," he said, stepping to the rail as an odd thickness filled his throat. Sam's presence enhanced the view considerably. The breeze caught her curls, twisting them in the moonlight like licking copper flames teasing her face. Until now he hadn't realized how dramatic her profile was—a straight nose, full, pouty lips, and a strong jaw that suggested a streak of stubbornness.

He hoped she wouldn't be bullheaded about giving up her criminal career.

Goofus planted his front paws on the deck railing next to her, his shaggy tail semaphoring his pleasure at having company after being abandoned all evening.

As she gave the dog a scratch between his ears, Sam said, "I can't imagine why anyone would ever leave this view, even for a few minutes. It's incredible."

"Nothing a few million dollars can't buy. But don't worry. As soon as we find you a suitable husband, he'll have enough money to buy you any view you'd like."

She shot him a look sparked with fireworks. "That's certainly very thoughtful of you."

"I'm basically a nice guy," he conceded, "and I don't want to see you make a mistake that will ruin your future. Just put yourself in my hands. I'll take care of all the details."

"Who would have believed I'd be so lucky as to have you for a big brother?"

"That's my girl." He placed his palm on her bare back and a sensation that wasn't at all brotherly shot up his arm, and had an interesting effect on other parts of his anatomy, as well. Shocked by his reaction, he removed his hand as if he'd been burned. "It's getting late. We'd better turn in."

"I suppose I need my beauty sleep if I'm going to

start meeting all these eligible men you have in mind tomorrow.''

''Yeah, well, we might not exactly start our campaign tomorrow. It may take a little more planning than that.'' This little project would take lots more planning than finding a home for a couple of oversize puppies and require far more care, he realized, as he began to backpedal at the prospect. *What man would be worthy of Sam Sterling?* he wondered.

''I'm a difficult case, huh?''

''No, I didn't mean that. It's just that—'' He mentally sorted through the Malibu crowd. Wealthy or not, at the moment he couldn't think of any guy who seemed right for Sam. She deserved someone special to give her all the things she'd missed as a kid. Someone capable of commitment. ''It's just that picking out a few prospects is going to take a little thought.''

As she went back inside, Sam seethed. Rogan must think she was a real dog. How hard could it be to introduce her to a few of his wealthy cronies? Did he think he'd have to bribe one to take her out?

And then she remembered that the whole idea of his matchmaking was totally absurd. She was here to find out if he had anything to do with the jewelry thefts in town, not to catch a husband. For all she knew, he could be running a whole syndicate of thieves right from this upscale Malibu hideaway.

As she passed the breakfast bar, she noticed the red light was still blinking on his answering machine, and it looked like there was more than one message—a whole bevy of Marijoes, she suspected grimly.

''Aren't you going to check your messages?'' she asked.

"It's late. They'll keep till tomorrow." With an indifferent shrug, he led her upstairs. In the hallway, he said, "Hang on a second while I see what I can find for you to wear."

He vanished behind a door and when he reappeared he was carrying a sheer teddy that was so skimpy it didn't even qualify as a garment.

"My, you certainly are prepared for overnight guests," Sam said dryly.

"Living in Malibu, you never know when you're going to get stuck here because of a landslide or brush fire that closes the highway, or even high waves. I like to be ready for any and all emergencies."

"I just bet you do, Rogan." He probably had a case of condoms on hand, too. Strictly for emergencies.

"If you don't like this, I'd be happy to lend you one of my T-shirts."

*Some choice,* she groused silently. "The T-shirt will do fine, thanks."

A minute later he produced the promised T-shirt— a stencilled one from a 10K race—and showed her a room with a queen-size bed and a view of the curving Santa Monica Bay.

"The bathroom's at the end of the hall. You'll find a new toothbrush in the drawer beside the sink and towels are in the cupboard. Anything else you need, just give a shout."

Her ever-gracious host departed and she blew out a sigh. By far, this was the craziest situation she could have gotten herself into. Surely other police officers didn't end up in some guy's house on their first undercover assignment, half expecting him to jump her bones...and half wanting him to. She couldn't remember a thing in the handbook that provided contingencies for this predicament.

She supposed at age thirteen she'd had no idea what her infatuation with Rogan would have meant, *if* she'd been able to act on those feelings. Now she did. All too clearly.

A few minutes later she'd turned off the light, curled up under the covers and was adjusting the fluffy pillow when she heard a sound at her door— little more than a soft knock.

"Well, I'll be..." she muttered. All along he'd been planning to get into her bed.

A frisson of excitement raced through her.

She'd fight him off, of course. She had the training. She wouldn't even need her weapon, which she'd slipped into the drawer of the bedside table.

The door edged open. Soft footfalls on the carpet crossed the floor to the side of the bed.

With the sound of heavy breathing coming ever closer, the bed groaned under the weight of the new arrival.

"Goofus? What are you doing here?" Sam resettled herself to make room for her furry bedmate, telling herself she was absolutely not disappointed that the intruder in her bedroom was an oversize mutt and not his master.

AFTER HE CHECKED his messages from the upstairs phone and made one early morning call, the steady thunk-thunk of his rowing machine lured Rogan downstairs. Tail wagging, Goofus followed along beside him. Rogan hadn't expected Sam to be up yet, much less working out on his gym equipment.

Nor had he expected her to look so damn sexy.

Great legs! Long and shapely and well-tanned in spite of her fair complexion. Solid, too. Cellulite was not a problem for Sam. He knew that because with her sitting down, the T-shirt she'd borrowed just barely reached the top of her thighs.

What had happened to the skinny, awkward adolescent he remembered? The one he'd loved to tease.

In her place he found a woman who made his palms itch to test the velvety-smooth texture of those legs. A woman who had insinuated her presence into a series of erotic dreams during the night.

He frowned. Maybe being a surrogate big brother was going to be tougher than he'd thought.

But that's what she needed—someone to watch out for her and keep her out of trouble. Not a man who had sex on his mind and couldn't handle commitment.

Instead he needed to concentrate on what a smart kid she'd been—and probably still was. And how good she'd been with the younger children who had lived in the neighborhood while they were growing up. And how she'd always stood her ground when he'd teased her, often giving as good as she got.

Yes, he needed to remember all those things—and forget about lust.

"Good morning," he said, renewing his resolve to do what was right. "You about ready for breakfast?"

She slowed the pace of her workout and turned to look up at him. Sweat sheened her face and, without a trace of makeup, she glowed with raging good health. It was hard to imagine any woman looking more beautiful. Or desirable. "If you're fixing it. I don't cook."

Goofus tried to plant a kiss on her face. With a laugh as light as the first rays of sunshine over the sea, she ducked and batted him away.

"You don't? I remember your mother made great waffles. And her homemade pizza was the best."

"Think of it as my way of rebelling." Standing, she picked up a towel that had been draped over the weight-lifting bench and wiped her face. Damp curls clung to her neck; the shirt clung to her breasts, the shadow of rosy nipples apparent.

Rogan's mouth went dry and he swallowed hard. He hoped the clothes he'd ordered for her showed up in a hurry. Then again, if Martin hadn't picked them up yet, maybe he could still order her a nun's habit.

"I've decided the three major food groups should be microwave, takeout, and any place I can make reservations," she told him, her eyes sparkling, her hand absently petting the dog. "Assuming somebody else is picking up the check."

His lips quirked into a smile as he reflected that her figure didn't show any ill effects from her unhealthy eating habits. "Will an omelet do? Cheese, onions, peppers and some salsa over the top."

"Sounds great." She hooked the towel around her neck. "Just for the record, I don't do windows, either."

"Determined not to follow in your mother's footsteps?"

"I made it a point to choose a different career."

"Oh? Is stealing jewels a sideline or a full-time occupation?"

"That crack doesn't deserve an answer, Rogan. We all know who had those diamond earrings in his pocket last night."

"Which I found in your purse," he told her.

"You what?" Sam's jaw went slack and her forehead tightened with a frown.

"I spotted security moving in and figured out what was going on. I checked your purse. So you wouldn't get caught, I ditched the diamonds by the auction table so nobody would be the wiser."

Something didn't compute, Sam decided. She'd been so sure Rogan had lifted the earrings and then had second thoughts. There was no way those gems could have ended up in her purse. Which she'd left on the table untended, she realized with an inaudible groan. *Stupid* mistake.

But why would anyone plant the diamonds in *her* purse? Unless it had been done in error.

As he headed for the kitchen, Rogan asked, "Where's your mother now?"

She did a double take at the rapid switch in topic.

Following him as far as the high breakfast bar that separated the cooking from the dining area, she pulled out a stool and sat down. Goofus parked himself by his dish in an alcove next to the refrigerator, a silly, almost human expression of expectation on his face.

"Mom moved to Idaho and started a cleaning business of her own a few years ago. She wanted to get away from the high crime rate here in L.A." Though Sam's mother had never personally been a victim of any crime, she'd become increasingly terrified by the daily news reports of drive-by shootings and by Sam's own near miss. So, like a lot of other people, she'd fled. "A year ago she was mugged right outside a grocery store in broad daylight."

"She okay?"

"She's fine. But she's thinking of moving again, for all the good that would do."

"Can't get away from it, can you?"

"Nope." Sam's answer had been to stay and fight the bad guys. She wasn't sure her current assignment would accomplish much. A man who chopped peppers and onions so deftly didn't seem like much of a threat to society, thief or not.

The way his shirt hung open, revealing a well-muscled chest roughened by a smattering of dark hair, was doing things to her libido, however. So did the fact that he hadn't managed to snap the top button of his cutoffs, leaving them clinging precariously to his lean hips and tantalizing her imagination. His hair was rumpled from sleep, all mussed walnut-brown strands that begged to be finger-combed by a woman; his whisker-shadowed cheeks invited her caress.

Damn if he didn't look better this morning than he had in his tux.

She'd done a quick search of the downstairs before he had gotten up and hadn't found anything incriminating. Maybe Garcia was wrong. Maybe she was on a wild goose chase trying to prove Rogan was involved in the thefts. She was definitely beginning to hope so.

Or maybe her judgment was clouded by adolescent memories and a nice pair of pecs.

THEY WERE WORKING on their second cup of coffee, a particularly aromatic blend, when the doorbell rang.

With an excited bark, Goofus made a beeline for the door, tail wagging.

Sam shot Rogan a look. "I'm not exactly dressed for company. I'd better—"

"Stay put. It's a delivery. He won't come in."

Rogan headed for the door and she heard a brief exchange, a masculine voice. He returned a moment later loaded down with shopping bags from an exclusive shop on Rodeo Drive. He dropped them onto the couch.

"I figured you'd need a change of clothes," he said by way of explanation.

"You didn't have to do that. I could have gone home."

"Maybe I didn't want you to go yet."

"Oh?" Tension tightened in her midsection. What was he up to now?

"A woman who carries a piece strapped to her leg piques my interest. Would you like to explain why you do that, Sam?"

The sip of coffee she'd just taken stuck in her throat. Her eyes watered and she choked. "Not particularly."

"Look, Sam, I'm trying to help you and I can't if you're not honest with me." He sauntered across the room, pulled out a bar stool and sat next to her—knee to knee. "Come on, Carrot Top. Tell me the truth."

She needed time to figure out what was going on, and who the real thief was, so she decided to play along. She'd tell him what he was prepared to hear, although lying didn't come easily to her. Particularly where Rogan was concerned. He *had* been a friend when she'd needed one, though she'd been too young to appreciate the flaws that came with the package. "You've got me dead to rights, Rogan. I am...husband hunting."

His dark eyebrows shot up.

"I figured if I hung around a place like the Beverly Hills Hotel I'd meet some wealthy men. Then, if I played my cards right, things would work out. I didn't much like growing up the housekeeper's daughter." That much, at least, was entirely true, and the lack of acceptance she'd experienced still stuck like a chicken bone in her throat.

"And you're supporting your star search by stealing jewels?"

"No. I didn't take those earrings, Rogan. I don't know how they got into my purse. I sincerely wish I did."

He wanted to believe her. She could see it in the slight tightening around his lips, the sympathy in his eyes. Better a gold digger than a jewel thief. But he was skeptical, too. That was obvious in the unconscious way he rubbed his thumb against the side of his finger. Measuring her credibility.

"And that gun you keep tucked away?" he asked.

She shrugged. "These days a girl has to be ready to protect herself."

He held her gaze steadily. He didn't act like a thief. But that might be the biggest *act* of all, Oscar caliber. Even so, she could have melted into those blue eyes of his. They were almost hypnotic in their intensity. She'd thought so ten years ago, and still did.

A phone rang and they both jumped.

Rogan swung around to answer the wall phone. But

even as he picked it up, the phone rang again. He stared at the instrument incredulously.

Muttering a curse, Sam hopped off the bar stool. "It's mine," she said, crossing the room to where she'd left her cell phone.

Irritated that anyone would call her on the police-issued phone while she was undercover, she snapped it open. "Yes?"

"Sam, it's me. Jackson."

"You shouldn't have called me here."

"The emeralds that were stolen a couple of weeks ago have shown up."

"Oh?"

"In Bakersfield. The guy who bought them remembers a man with a British accent. From the description, it could be Geoffrey Hughes."

"That's interesting." She met Rogan's curious gaze from across the room.

Bobby said, "Hughes and Prescott have been friends for a long time, Sam. They might be in this together."

Sam didn't want to believe that. She really didn't. But she was a cop. Anything was possible. "I'd rather you didn't call me here again."

"Garcia wants you to stick as close to Prescott as you can. The precise wording of his order I'm not willing to repeat."

"I can imagine."

"Watch your step, Sam."

Without responding, she snapped the phone closed. "Sorry for the interruption," she told Rogan.

"Your partner, I take it."

"In a manner of speaking."

"I gather he's not suitable husband material."

"Definitely not." He already had a wife and a three-month-old baby, and she wasn't exactly fond of him anyway.

"Then I'm glad you told him to get lost." He speared his fingers through his mussed hair. "Why don't you try on the clothes I had Aunt Agatha's chauffeur pick up for you? Martin usually has pretty good taste. And I think we'd better get started right away on our little project."

She bristled. "I'm not a charity case, Rogan. And I'm not a stray. I have a home and clothes of my own."

"Just do it, Sam. You aren't the first woman to set your sights on snaring a wealthy husband. My job is to be sure you aim at the right one."

*Her* job was to stick as closely to Rogan as she could.

Swallowing a few choice words she wanted to hurl at Rogan—*and* Garcia, now that she thought of it— Sam snatched up the clothes. She couldn't very well wander around Malibu all day in her fancy cocktail dress. But she didn't have to like being ordered around by a couple of bossy men, particularly when one of them had the uncanny ability to slip past emotional barricades she'd constructed years ago.

# Chapter Four

Body stretched full length, Sam dived for the ball, saved it and ate a mouthful of sand. She came up sputtering, pleased one of her teammates had nailed her setup and spiked it back over the net to the opposition.

She cheered. "Way to go, Jason!"

"That's game point!" Grinning, he offered her a high-five, along with the third member of their team, Buddy Something, who lived about three houses down from Rogan. "You're terrific, Sam. Where'd you learn to play like that?"

"I went to college on a volleyball scholarship."

"No fooling? That's great!"

On the opposite side of the net, Rogan grumbled, "It figures." Sweat beaded his forehead and dripped down the center line of his chest, dampening an intriguing swirl of dark hair that arrowed below his waistband. His arms hung limply at his sides in defeat. He was breathing hard from his futile effort to handle the well-placed spike. Not that he was responsible for his team's loss. For an amateur, he was amazingly athletic and quite skilled.

Sam manfully tried, and failed, to suppress a victorious smile.

Sensing a lull in the action, Goofus entered center ring, leaping up to snap at the net. When it fluttered back at him, he raced for cover.

Everyone laughed.

"Hey, losers buy the beer. Right, Rogan?" Buddy asked.

"Sure." He thumbed over his shoulder toward his house. "You know where to find it."

"Wore you out, did we?"

"Not in your lifetime, Buddy."

While Buddy went to get the beer, the other players milled around. Rogan left the makeshift court and plopped himself down on the steps to his house. Sam joined him.

Goofus loyally sprawled at Rogan's feet.

"I like your friends," she said. She leaned her elbows on the step above her, tipped her head back and squinted up into the bright sky. It was a terrific Sunday afternoon, true Southern California weather with a lazy breeze blowing in from the ocean. Her fellow officers at the West L.A. police station would not view this as a bad assignment, she mused. At the moment, she tended to agree.

"I didn't know you were such a jock," Rogan commented.

She shrugged. "I've always been good at sports."

"Like climbing trees, as I recall."

She smiled, remembering the big sprawling oak in the Prescott backyard, and how Rogan had climbed up to sit next to her when she'd felt terribly alone—

deserted by her father, whom she'd never seen again. "I've mostly given that up in my old age."

"Hmm. Just as well. I was always afraid you were going to break your neck. Of course, now that you're all grown up, you might keep in mind as we check out possible husband prospects that some men find an athletic woman a little intimidating. It's hard on a man's ego to get wiped out by a woman at a game like volleyball."

"Oh? Don't tell me losing this pickup game damaged your ego."

"Me? No, not at all." Shaking his head, he shifted his position so he was facing her, leaning on one elbow. His knee brushed against her thigh, sending a shiver of awareness up her leg. *Sexual awareness.* "In fact, I'm impressed. I like a strong woman. But sometimes my friends can be real dolts."

"I see." She gritted her teeth.

"I just wanted to point out—"

"In brotherly fashion?"

"Yeah. There might be some guys who would be put off by—"

"Jason and Buddy didn't seem to mind my help beating you and the others."

"Well, no, of course not. But that doesn't mean they'd be interested in—"

"Marriage."

"That's right. I'm glad you understand."

Sam understood, all right. He was saying she wasn't acceptable in his social set. She fumed at the put-down and remembered all the hurts she'd experienced in school. If she had her way, next time Rogan's team wouldn't win a single point. The poor baby's ego be damned!

Jogging down the steps, Buddy arrived with a six pack. He stepped gingerly between Rogan and Sam, and over Goofus, who let out an uncharacteristic growl of warning.

Eyeing the dog, Buddy offered Sam the first beer, took one himself, then placed the remaining cans on the post at the foot of the stairs. With a scowl, Rogan reached up to claim one for himself.

"So you're visiting for a while?" Buddy asked Sam in an easy conversational opener as he popped the tab on his beer can. A stocky man, he looked more like a rugby player than someone who'd be good at volleyball.

"My aunt asked me to look out for her," Rogan interjected.

"That so?" Buddy glanced from Sam to Rogan. "Does that mean you don't have any claim on this pretty lady?"

Sam flushed. "*No one* has a claim on me, Buddy."

"Great. Then how 'bout dinner tonight?"

Whoa, he was quick! Which gave Sam's ego a much-needed boost after Rogan's disparaging remarks.

Rogan shoved himself to his feet. Leaner than Buddy, he was also several inches taller, his stance decidedly confrontational. "Sorry. She has other plans."

"I do?"

He shot her a silencing look. "Yeah, you do."

Odd behavior, she mused. But she didn't particularly want to go out with Buddy anyway. He seemed nice enough but he wasn't... Well, he wasn't on her list of suspects, she rationalized, and she was here to investigate the jewel thefts, not to socialize. And certainly not to find a husband.

Buddy raised one hand in surrender, the other still occupied holding a beer. "Hey, I didn't mean to poach. All you needed to do was say so." He winked at Sam. "Maybe I'll check with you later when your guard dog isn't around."

Sam wasn't entirely sure whether he meant Goofus or Rogan. She suspected the latter, particularly since Rogan had visibly tensed. He was all but growling.

As Buddy wandered off, Sam popped the tab on her beer can and took a sip. The smooth, cool liquid felt good sliding down her parched throat. "What was that all about?" she asked Rogan.

A pair of frown lines deepened across his forehead. "Buddy's not right for you."

"He wasn't proposing. He just wanted to go out with me."

"One thing can lead to another. No sense wasting your time on a loser."

"Loser? In your lexicon, does that mean his bank account runs to less than seven figures?"

"Not exactly."

He glanced away evasively, making Sam wonder if he was lying to her. And why he would bother to do that.

But when she followed his gaze, she spotted a pair of young women jogging along the beach toward them. They were both perfect prototypical California girls with long blond hair, hourglass figures and sun-bronzed bodies that would have been indecently exposed except for two minuscule pieces of fabric that masqueraded as swimsuits—and, Sam was confident, had never been dampened by so much as a drop of saltwater.

One of the girls waved. "Hi, guys. The party's at our place next Saturday. See you then?"

"You bet, Louanne," Buddy called back to them. "Wouldn't miss it."

Every male on the beach, their tongues practically touching their toes, watched as the girls jogged by, effectively advertising the fringe benefits of attending their weekend event.

Forcefully reminding herself that the social scene in Malibu was none of her concern, Sam said to Rogan, "I appreciate your generous hospitality and all your brotherly attention, but I'd really like to go home and pick up a few of my things. Maybe check my mail. And get my car." She hated being dependent on anyone for transportation and she'd taken a taxi to the charity event last night to avoid Rogan picking her up. In the current circumstances, she felt very much trapped.

Cocking a single, well-arched brow, he slid her a glance. "Where do you live?"

"A small rent-controlled duplex in Santa Monica," she admitted, still reluctant to let him know too much about her personal life.

"You, uh, live alone?"

"Of course I do. What did you expect?"

An unfamiliar knot of tension eased from between Rogan's shoulder blades. He wasn't quite sure what he had expected but he was relieved that "partner" of hers who had called that morning wasn't her room-mate.

Funny that that would bother him. It was stranger still that he had practically jumped down Buddy's throat when the guy had asked Sam to dinner. The whole idea had been to fix her up with some wealthy friend who'd make an honest woman of her. Buddy, one of the rising stars in the brokerage business, was worth megabucks.

He was also a ladies' man who'd had a parade of young, voluptuous women like Louanne and her friend Betsy moving in and out of his place down the beach, changing faces almost as fast as the tide shifted. Hell, Rogan didn't want Sam to get hooked up with a guy like that. And he sure didn't understand women who got themselves caught in that kind of a revolving door.

Besides, he hadn't liked the way Buddy and the other guys had ogled Sam's long legs and slender figure, shown off to perfection in shorts that were a bit too tight. Nor had he appreciated their lingering looks on her skimpy halter top. There'd only been one thing on their minds.

It hadn't been volleyball.

Next time he asked his aunt's chauffeur to make clothing selections for Sam, he'd request nothing more revealing than a muumuu.

THE ONE-STORY STUCCO duplex was several miles in-land from the beach in a neighborhood of older homes. Even the most fearless skate-boarder would have been challenged by the undulating sidewalks, raised at odd angles by the roots of the giant trees that arched over the street.

Rogan parked at the curb. Though it wasn't a bad place to live, he could understand why she might want to upgrade to something a little fancier.

"No question about it," he said. "Staying at my place is a better choice. You'll have a much better chance of meeting the right man than you would living here."

The look Sam shot him was full of fury and he wondered why. He was simply trying to help her out. He understood how money attracted money. He'd seen it happen dozens of times among his buddies—and then their marriages failed and they were back to being gadabout bachelors again.

That particular thought was damn discouraging. He'd have to be careful about who he selected for Sam.

"Thanks for bringing me home," she said tautly. "I won't be long. I'll just pack a few things so I'll be *properly* attired for my coming-out season in Malibu." She shoved open the car door as though she was hopping mad. He didn't know why.

But a serious dose of curiosity gave him a nudge. "I'll walk you to your door."

"You don't have to do that."

But he wanted to. So he got out of the car to follow her.

When she turned to go up the walkway, a small child came running out to greet her. She had strawberry-blond curls that danced as she flew into Sam's welcoming arms.

"You're home!" the child cried.

"You bet I am, sweetie." Sam gave the youngster a huge hug and lifted her onto her hip as if she'd done it a thousand times before—like a mother would do.

My God! Sam had a kid?

The possibility slammed into Rogan's gut like a railroad train. She hadn't mentioned... He'd had no idea...

The little girl looked in Rogan's direction. "Who's he?" the child asked Sam.

"That's Rogan. He brought me home."

"Is he gonna be your new boyfriend?"

"Not a chance." She eyed Rogan, her glare still sharply angry. "He's more like a pushy big brother."

"He's cute."

Gratified to hear her description, Rogan gave the kid a tentative smile. "Yours?" he asked Sam casually.

Sam looked at him blankly. "You think Tessa is *my* child?"

"Well, her hair's kind of red, and I thought maybe..." He jammed his hands into his pockets. He didn't know quite what to think. Sam *had* told him she lived alone, he belatedly recalled.

"Tessa is my neighbor's little girl. Sometimes she lets me baby-sit her."

"Only when you've been very, very good," the child said solemnly.

Sam gave Tessa another squeeze and set her down. The little girl went running toward another woman who had just stepped out the front door of the second unit—a woman with strawberry-blond hair pulled back in a ponytail.

Rogan pressed out a breath of air. Sam had looked so damn natural with a child in her arms, he'd assumed...and he'd been consumed with a rare stab of envy, a roaring desire that Sam's child should be his, not some other man's. An absurd thought, he realized even as it popped into his head. "I guess I jumped to a wrong conclusion."

"You certainly did. Marilyn's my neighbor and a good friend. She's a single mom because her husband ducked out on her when she was six months pregnant with Tessa."

"That's rough."

"No worse than when my father left my mother when I was seven. It's never been easy to raise a child alone. And at least Tessa won't be sitting on the porch for a year waiting for her father to come home."

"Is that what you did?"

A shocked expression came over Sam's face as though she hadn't realized how much pain she'd revealed with those few words. But Rogan remembered how troubled she'd been when she'd moved to his parents' house. A father's desertion wasn't something a kid got over easily, he imagined, recalling his father had always been a part of the household if not exactly attentive to either his wife or his children.

She shrugged. "It was a long time ago."

Rogan suspected that when she allowed herself to think about it, the emotions were as raw today as they had been fifteen years ago. He pictured her shortly after she'd moved into the housekeeper's quarters on the Prescott estate. She'd been sitting on the branch of a climbing tree. Sad. Alone. And all he'd wanted to do was make her smile.

"Look, Rogan, why don't you go on back to Malibu?"

"You are going to come back, aren't you? To my place. So I can help you find the right husband."

She studied him for several impossibly long heartbeats and he couldn't read her expression. But he did know he very much wanted her to say yes. And it shouldn't have mattered so much.

"Maybe I've got it all wrong," he said, his voice thickening with an emotion he was reluctant to name. "Maybe you've got some terrific job and they wouldn't want you to take any time off."

"No, no one is likely to miss me," she admitted. Finally, her expression more resigned than enthusiastic, she said, "I'll come back to your place. Give me an hour or two to get myself organized."

A combined sense of relief and pleasure swept through him with surprising potency.

"WHO WAS THAT GUY?" Marilyn Justice echoed her daughter's earlier question.

Sam quickly sorted through her mail before dropping it on her kitchen table. Nothing but bills and junk mail. "He's a friend."

"He's a hunk who kept you out all night, if I'm any judge."

Heat crept up her neck. "It's not what you think."

"Don't tell me he's a cop? A new partner? If he is, I'm gonna go get myself arrested. Maybe I could rob a bank or something."

In spite of herself, Sam laughed. "No, he's not on the force. And he doesn't know I am, so don't mention it if he happens to come around again." Which

Sam certainly hoped he wouldn't. It'd be too easy to have her cover blown if he lingered in the neighborhood. The fact that he had effortlessly ferreted out her Achilles' heel, her deep sense of betrayal at her father's abandonment, wasn't an issue. Rogan was still a suspect in a major rash of jewel thefts.

And her boss wanted her stuck like glue to the man.

She opened the refrigerator, took out an opened half gallon of milk and handed it to Marilyn. "I'm going to be gone for a few days—"

"With him?"

"Well, yes—"

"I knew it! You're having an affair."

"I don't believe in casual affairs and that's the only kind—"

"Oh, go ahead. It'd be good for you. And he's crazy about you, I can tell."

"You can?" Admittedly, Rogan made her heart skip a beat easily enough, but he only thought of her as his little sister. Probably a pesky one at that, who could beat him at volleyball. And he wanted to find her a *husband,* of all the arrogant, impossible—

"He's got dreamy eyes and they were all over you. I'd go for it, if I were you."

"He's the last guy on earth I'd consider marrying." His family's history of infidelity definitely put him out of the running. Not that she had anyone else in mind at the moment. And he had a whole flock of women to choose from, no doubt putting her at the bottom of his list, as well.

"Who's talking marriage? I'm talkin' hot in the sack. Intimate aerobics. He'd be dynamite."

It took little imagination to believe that statement.

At least from Sam's point of view she could certainly picture some athletic moves on Rogan's part. And hers. Assuming he lost interest in this big brother, matchmaking bit and could squeeze her into his busy social schedule.

"I don't know how you can even suggest such a thing, Marilyn. Not after the way your husband dumped you. Men can be so unreliable."

"So I made a mistake with David." She shrugged. "That doesn't mean I want to dry up and turn into an old prune. Trust me, hon, if a hunk like that gave me a second look, I'd give it a shot. You should, too."

"I don't know," she said slowly.

"Every girl needs at least one fling before she settles down. Why not him?"

A thousand reasons should have popped into Sam's head. None did.

Surely she'd think of one later.

"Look, you've got my cell phone number," Sam said. "And I'll leave you his address in case anything important comes up."

"Honey, it would take a disaster of major proportions before I'd think of interfering with your little tête-à-tête with that hunk. You're on your own. Enjoy!"

"You'll look after my plants?"

"Like they were my own," she pledged. "For as long as it takes."

Her cheeks flushing furiously, Sam shooed her friend out of the duplex. Marilyn had it all wrong. Rogan Prescott was at the absolute bottom of her list of men she wanted to have an affair with.

Not that there were any other men on *that* list, either, she realized grimly. None of her fellow police officers had appealed to her, and the only other men she'd met lately were felons or cons. She really needed to do something about her social life—and she would, just as soon as she was through with this case, she vowed.

After packing a few changes of clothes—the nicest ones she owned—she was on her way back to Malibu. En route to her undercover assignment, she reminded herself. She could almost see Detective Garcia glowering at her, ready to pounce with a "Listen up, *Officer* Sterling" if she messed up her end of the investigation.

That wasn't going to happen.

If Rogan was involved in the jewel thefts, she'd nail him. What Marilyn had said—and whatever growing, or renewed, personal feelings she might have for Rogan—wouldn't get in her way.

CAUGHT in a bumper-to-bumper jam of Sunday drivers, Sam inched her way along Pacific Coast Highway, finally taking her life into her hands when she turned across the traffic into Rogan's driveway. She squeezed into a space next to an unfamiliar car, a brand new Porsche.

Once she survived Goofus's warm licks of welcome, she discovered Geoffrey sitting on the back deck reading a newspaper.

Yep! That's why she shouldn't consider having an affair with Rogan. A cop needed to keep an emotional distance from suspects. *And* their friends.

When she slid open the screen door, Geoffrey looked up.

"There you are!" he said, beaming her a friendly smile. "Rogan said you were staying with him. Good show, I say. He's a good lad, though I wish you had given me a go first. Suppose I should have moved quicker, but we British can be a bit slow off the mark. Good for the long haul, though."

Sam wasn't at all sure how to react to Geoffrey's comment. Anything she said was likely to be misconstrued, so she opted for a little subtle interrogation.

"What brings you down to the beach?" she asked.

"Thought I might be able to entice Rogan into a small investment, but so far it's a no-go. Instead he decided to take a run down the beach. Apparently he doesn't see the value of having Pacific Rim trading partners as clearly as I do."

"It's certainly an area of growing commercial interest," she said, wondering what the going rate was for stolen gems. Pretty high, she imagined. An appropriate avenue for capital investment for a man who thought of himself as a wheeler-dealer. "What were you thinking about trading?"

"This and that. Whatever is likely to turn a profit." He snapped open the newspaper, and she realized it was the *Wall Street Journal.* "There's more to the Orient than simply cheap labor, you know. Here's an article on the booming franchising businesses around the rim. Even in mainland China. Fascinating, don't you think?"

Actually, Sam did find it interesting as Geoffrey waxed on about various financial opportunities in the Far East. She pulled a chair around to sit, deciding

he was more intelligent than she had previously suspected. That didn't make him an innocent man, of
course. He could still be using the proceeds from
jewel thefts to fund legitimate businesses. But his
comments were quite engrossing.

So much so that she didn't notice when Rogan returned.

"It won't work, Geoffrey."

Both she and Geoffrey turned at the sound of Rogan's voice.

He was standing at the top of the deck steps. Obviously returning from a run on the beach, a vee of
sweat darkening the fabric of his gray, cut-off T-shirt.
His muscular arms glistened and his hair was damp,
curling at his forehead and at his nape. His midriff
was bare and the sight far more fascinating than any
discussion of intellectual property rights or trade
wars.

With an effort, Sam forced herself to swallow the
sigh that threatened.

"What won't work, old man?" Geoffrey asked.

"Even if you convince Sam you've got a great
idea, I invest my money here at home."

"A flag waver, are you?"

"And proud of it. Sorry, *old man.*" Rogan added
plenty of emphasis on the "old man," though Geoff
wasn't much older than he was. Rogan simply didn't
like how cozy Geoff and Sam had looked together.
Who would have guessed she knew so much about
tariffs and trade barriers? Sam kept providing him
with one surprise after the other, not the least of
which was how possessive he felt about her. In a

*brotherly* way, he assured himself. Except that little detail was getting harder and harder to remember.

"Seems to me you said you had plans for this evening, Geoffrey," Rogan said pointedly. He hefted himself up to sit on the deck railing, his back to the setting sun. "Sam and I won't mind if you have to leave now."

Geoffrey cocked a faint brow. "Right-o! I know when I'm not wanted." With good grace, he scooped up his newspaper, bowed gallantly to Sam, and left through the house.

Rogan frowned at Sam. "What was your major in college? Business?"

"No, I—" Sam clamped her mouth shut. She'd almost given away her police science major. "General studies."

"You seem to know a lot about foreign trade issues."

"I have been known to read a newspaper now and then."

"Admirable. Just keep in mind a guy—even someone like Geoffrey—likes to think he's smarter than a woman."

"Is that how you feel?"

"No. Not me. Just the opposite." He dropped to the deck, not even wanting to consider that Geoffrey might have more than a passing interest in Sam. And appalled he'd made such a dumb comment. But when he'd spotted Sam with Geoffrey, he'd seen red. Or maybe the color had been green, as in *green* with envy. Whatever was happening, Rogan knew he was acting a little crazy. He couldn't seem to stop himself.

"I admire intelligence in a woman. I just think if you're going to catch a man—"

"I have to act stupid?"

"Well, it could pay off if you made the guy *think* he had some smarts compared to you. If you made him feel important."

"Because of his fragile ego."

"Something like that."

Fuming, Sam stood. If her job didn't depend on cracking this case, she'd let Rogan know exactly what she thought of his archaic reasoning. This was not the Victorian era. A woman was allowed to have brains. And athletic ability.

"I'm going to go unpack," she said tautly.

"Great. I'll shower and then I'll start dinner. Steak and salad okay with you?"

"Perfect," she snapped, turning away. There was no reason on earth why this insufferable man's attitude about women in general—and her in particular—should hurt so much. But it did.

And while he was occupied in the kitchen, she was damn well going to take a look around upstairs. If there was so much as a speck of diamond dust up there, she'd find it.

No DOUBT ABOUT IT. Rogan was a whiz around the kitchen. The succulent steak practically melted in Sam's mouth, the light seasonings enhancing the flavor rather than overwhelming it. The caesar salad boasted ice-cold, perfectly crisp lettuce and a smooth, tangy dressing. The croutons were superbly fresh and crunchy.

She sighed. He'd make some hardworking woman a terrific wife.

And if his sideline was stealing jewels, he certainly covered his tracks well. She hadn't been able to find anything out of the ordinary—except for that sexy teddy he kept for emergencies.

She hated to think about how many women had worn it. Or had Rogan remove it for them, she thought with an even more discouraged sigh.

As they sat at the dining table, a cool breeze danced through the screen door, flickering the candles. The sound of the ocean caressing the beach was like a finely tuned orchestra. To avoid focusing on Rogan or thinking about the way his dark hair caught the gleam of the candlelight, Sam concentrated on the paintings he had on display.

"I don't know a thing about art," she admitted. "How do you decide which paintings you want to buy?"

"I look for something that moves me. A spark, I suppose you could call it. A distinctive style."

He sipped his wine, his gaze very intensely directed at her, not on the paintings. It made Sam feel as though she was being measured by the same yardstick. She wondered how she was doing.

"The picture behind me was done by a young artist who's in a wheelchair. She uses a primitive style, but in every one of her paintings you can see her admiration for physical strength. Makes for an interesting combination."

"Yes, it does."

In fact, as Rogan discussed each of the paintings, Sam became increasingly fascinated by his passion for the subject. Juxtaposed with his easygoing, play-boy life-style, the contrast was quite startling—and intriguing. Once again she had to admit there was more depth to Rogan Prescott than she had previously suspected.

Granted, as a teenager he'd always taken time to say hello to her, even when there'd been a bevy of high school beauties hanging around him. And he'd fixed the flat tires on her bike more than once without complaint and only his usual dose of teasing. But he'd been so easygoing, she hadn't really seen his deeper side. Maybe she'd been too young to recognize it, or had been caught up in the adoration of an "older" man who would pay even a small amount of attention to her.

"Have you ever tried your own hand at painting?" she asked.

His full lips slid into an endearing grin. "To my instructor's everlasting regret."

"Maybe you have other talents." Like making a woman feel all soft and feminine, even when she doesn't want to.

"I won't deny that, but I'll leave the creative side of art to those who have the gift. There's nothing worse than a mediocre painting."

"But you must do something. I mean—" She made a sweeping gesture of his home. "Is all of this your inheritance?" Or do you cash in a diamond a week to support your life-style? she wanted to ask.

He seemed unconcerned by her personal question. "Just like finding good painters, I make investments in other businesses. Some of them have done quite well." He shrugged. "Others have cost me a bundle.

The fact is, if I worked at a real job I'd be taking money away from somebody else who needs it. So I guess I'm condemned to a lifetime of unemployment.''

He didn't appear the least unhappy with his lot in life as he stood to clear the table.

"I'll help you with the dishes," she volunteered as she got up, too. In spite of his casual attitude about not having a job, she wondered if it bothered him at some level, and then she quickly put the thought aside. Given his millions, why would he care about actually working?

They both reached for the same plate. Rogan's hands closed over hers as they lifted it together.

Heat spiraled up her arms and curled into her chest. His palms were warm and slightly rough, his scent a seductive combination of musk and spicy aftershave. Very masculine. Very appealing.

His eyes darkened and focused on her lips. The reflected flame of candlelight shone in their blue depths, like the deepest regions of the sea, beckoning the unwary to come a little closer. Tempting those too weak at heart to resist.

Sam swallowed hard. Unbidden, her tongue slipped out to moisten her lips.

He was going to kiss her.

Lord help her, that's just what she wanted.

Her heart stutter-stepped to a faster beat. Almost imperceptibly, she felt herself leaning toward him.

"Do you like to wash or dry?" he asked, his voice low and raspy. Tantalizingly intimate.

"It doesn't matter." Anticipation closed her throat, making her reply no more than a whisper.

"Great. I'll let you turn on the dishwasher after I get the dishes rinsed."

She blinked as he released her hands. "Oh." Swaying, her knees almost buckled at the sudden loss of his warm touch.

Damn him! He had no right to make her feel that way when she had absolutely no effect on him. It simply wasn't fair.

THE WEEK SPUN OUT and Sam and Rogan maintained their odd imitation of a couple living together. They talked but they didn't come close. They walked on the beach but they didn't touch.

He'd made no effort to introduce her to any more of his friends. For the most part, he ignored the blinking red light on his answering machine and the calls that were invariably from women.

On the beach, when women made it a point to seek him out, he was charming but noncommittal. Sam sensed every one of them went away disappointed.

Meanwhile Sam was unable to find a single clue in his house that might lead her to a stash of stolen jewels. Detective Garcia expressed his displeasure in no uncertain terms when she checked in at the station. The investigation appeared to be at a dead end.

She pleaded to be released from her assignment.

Garcia was adamant. "Listen up. Stick close to Prescott. We'll get a break soon."

The whole situation had very nearly driven Sam crazy by the time Sunday rolled around and they were en route to Aunt Agatha's famous brunch.

Martin, Agatha's butler and chauffeur, greeted them at the door.

"Good day, sir. Miss Sterling." He nodded slightly. "Madam has asked us to serve at poolside this morning."

Sam smiled at the butler's rigid posture and strong accent. As a child she'd known servants who loved to put on airs, pretending they worked for British royalty. She wondered if he was the real thing.

"Good day to have plenty of privacy and dignity," Agatha said as he went up politely from normal.

Sam shifted in her chair, Rogan brushed and swung against him. The chintz-covered sometimes who loved to have and understand they wanted to Battalions day. She wondered if he was the seat there.

# *Chapter Five*

"There you are, dear boy!" Agatha greeted Rogan in her customary effusive manner, including a kiss on the cheek. "And you've brought Samantha with you. How nice. What a pretty girl you are, my dear."

Sam colored like the first blush of sunrise. Rogan liked that about her, though he doubted she appreciated a trait that gave away her emotions so easily.

"It's kind of you to invite me," Sam said, allowing the older woman to peck her cheek, as well.

"I trust my nephew has been behaving himself."

"Like a perfect gentleman."

Agatha's eyes widened in surprise. "Mercy! That's not like Rogan at all!" Laughing, she hooked her arm through Sam's, leading her toward an umbrella-shaded table at poolside, one of three that awaited this morning's guests.

Grimly, Rogan agreed with his aunt's assessment. He had been acting with uncharacteristic restraint ever since he'd almost kissed Sam a week ago. Every day had become an endurance test to see if he could keep his hands off her for another twenty-four hours. Or even another minute.

Never in his life could he remember wanting a woman as much as he wanted Sam.

And never had his desire been more inappropriate.

Talk about lousy timing! He was supposed to be acting like a surrogate brother to her and helping her land a husband, somebody who'd keep her out of trouble.

With her sleeping right down the hall from him, all he kept thinking about—dreaming about—was how he'd like to get her between *his* sheets.

She deserved better than that, something more than a roll or two in the sack. But he knew his genetic limitations: Prescott men were notorious for their none-too-discreet philandering. Nothing suggested he would be any different if he made the mistake of committing to something as permanent as marriage.

He was thirty-one years old and never once had he met a woman he'd want to spend the rest of his life with. The fact was, his playboy reputation was severely exaggerated and mostly due to his dating a variety of women who rarely interested him past the third outing. Then he had to extricate himself from the relationship. Only once—that time in college— had he risked a longer relationship. And that had been devastating—for the woman.

Apparently that's how all the Prescotts were, their wives more social ornaments than long-term partners.

He couldn't put Sam in that position, even though he had to admit he'd never enjoyed a woman's company more. Given the pain she still carried because her father had walked out on his family, she didn't need to suffer the abuse of desertion a second time.

But damn, every time he thought of introducing her

to some other guy, he clutched. It was the same feeling he'd gotten as a kid whenever the high-jump bar had been raised beyond his personal best. He'd needed all of his guts to take that next running leap. He hadn't always made it.

For Sam, he'd simply have to find the courage.

AGATHA LED THEM to a table where Rogan's brother and sister-in-law were already seated. The day's attire was resort casual for both of them—sporty short-sleeve silk shirts and white pants. The woman wore a pair of gold hoop earrings that were not unlike Sam's.

"Sit here, dear boy," Agatha said, "and see if you can cheer up your brother. He's quite glum this morning, I'm afraid."

As Rogan made the introductions, Sam had a panicky moment thinking Adam might remember her from her years as the housekeeper's daughter. But there was no flicker of recognition in his eyes as they shook hands across the table. He'd been so much older than she, and so rarely home, he'd probably never noticed her.

His wife, Eileen, seemed distracted, hardly acknowledging the introduction.

"So what's up?" Rogan asked his brother.

"It looks like Eileen's the latest victim of the jewel thief that's been plaguing everyone."

Sam's interest perked up. "What did you lose?"

"It's terrible, really," Eileen said. As she glanced nervously at her husband, Sam was struck by the feeling this extraordinarily beautiful blonde was Adam's "trophy" wife, not someone he cherished.

"We were at the Montebanks' party last night. They're always dressed to the nine's, so I wanted to wear my diamonds." Her immaculately manicured hand fluttered to her throat.

"She should have left the damn things home," Adam grumbled. "They're worth a bloody fortune and with all the thefts we've been having lately, anyone with good sense—"

"I'm sorry," Eileen whispered. "I don't know what I was thinking. But they *are* insured."

Adam snorted derisively. "Thank God. My wife seems to think I'm some sort of a damn money tree."

"Did you call the police?" Sam asked sympathetically.

"They came, all right." Adam paused while an elderly maid dressed in a black uniform set compotes of fruit in front of each of them. "Not that the cops found anything. You'd think by now they'd have caught the crook. How stupid can the cops be, for God's sake?"

Sam bristled at the comment and felt her face flush.

"Maybe this thief is smarter than the usual crook," Rogan suggested. He slanted Sam a look. "At least Sam and I have alibis this time."

"Don't be so sure." She glanced at Eileen. "What time did you miss your jewels?"

"Oh, I don't know…" Her fingers danced another agitated path along her prominent breastbone, her long nails a striking shade of deep purple. She was so slender, she looked almost anorexic. "It was about one-thirty when Adam realized I wasn't wearing my necklace anymore."

"The damn thief lifted the necklace without Eileen

feeling a thing. The guy's good, I'll give him that,'' Adam muttered sourly.

Rogan dipped his fork into his fruit compote. "See? What did I tell you? Both Sam and I were at home sleeping when the theft happened."

"I was sleeping *alone*," Sam noted pointedly. "You could have left the house without my hearing you. And the necklace could have been stolen hours earlier without Eileen's knowledge."

Adam made a snickering noise. "You mean to tell me, little brother, that this beautiful woman's staying at your place and she's *not* sleeping in your bed? Boy, have you lost your touch!"

Rogan's ruddy cheeks deepened by several shades. "Watch it, Adam," he warned tautly.

"Oh, leave your brother alone," Eileen admonished. "All you ever think about when it comes to women is sex."

"What else is there?" Adam snapped.

Eileen ducked her head, concentrating on her fruit, her hand shaking slightly as she forked a piece of melon to her mouth.

Sam didn't like how this morning was going. The news of another theft was discouraging, particularly when she couldn't honestly account for Rogan's whereabouts. She'd have to check with Detective Garcia to see who else had been in attendance at the Montebank affair.

Maybe the field of suspects had narrowed.

She also didn't care for Adam's attitude about women or the police force. However impossible Rogan might be at times, at least he didn't share all of his brother's views. Just some of them, she thought in dismay.

While the butler made the rounds of the guests, refilling glasses of champagne or pouring coffee, the maid delivered plates heaped with thick slices of cinnamon French toast and crisp-cooked bacon.

"Thanks, Juanita," Rogan said.

"I knew you were coming this morning," the older woman confided with a sweet smile. "I told the missus you'd want French toast."

"I always do, if you're the one who makes it."

She giggled girlishly and moved off to serve the other guests.

"Is there any woman who doesn't fall for your charms?" Sam asked under her breath.

He shot her an all-too-cocky look. "Juanita has worked for Agatha for as long as I can remember. She probably came across the border as an illegal, but she's a citizen now. Votes every election, runs a tight ship around here, and takes really good care of Agatha. I've been proposing to her since I was about twenty so I could enjoy her French toast every morning, but she keeps turning me down."

In spite of herself, Sam laughed. Juanita was a very wise woman not to get mixed up with any of the Prescott men. They weren't good husband material. That much was abundantly clear.

A few minutes later, Agatha pulled up a chair at their table, apparently making the rounds of her guests.

"Now then," she said, "I promised to tell Samantha all about Chandler House, didn't I, dear?"

Adam groaned, "I suppose you're going to make the rest of us listen, too."

"Naturally." Agatha smiled brightly at her eldest nephew. "Your contributions have been so miserly this year, I intend to bore you until you're willing to give twice as much just to shut me up."

Eileen said, "I'd make a contribution but Adam keeps me on a very tight allowance. I'm sorry."

"No matter." Agatha waved off Eileen's apology with an impatient flick of her wrist, then proceeded to describe the refuge for ex-gang members that was so close to her heart.

As Agatha chattered on at length, Sam found herself enthralled with the woman's enthusiasm. Before she knew it, she said, "I'll send you a few dollars, Aunt Agatha. It won't be much but the cause does seem important." On a police officer's budget, her generosity would no doubt appear minuscule compared to even Adam's contribution.

"You do what you can, dear." She patted Sam's hand. "It's an investment in the future, you know. I have friends as far away as New York and Florida who've given."

"She twists arms wherever she goes," Rogan added good-naturedly.

"And I, for one," Adam said, "get plenty tired of it." He shoved back his chair and stood. "Come on, Eileen. I'm going to make some calls and see if I can build a fire under the police. There's no reason why they can't put a stop to this crime wave. What do they think we pay taxes for?"

Instead of simply telling Sam goodbye, Adam let

his hand rest on her shoulder. He squeezed gently. Suggestively.

"When you get tired of Rogan, give me a call," he said in a voice so low his brother couldn't hear him. "I promise to show you a good time. I'm an original ladies' man. They all love me, you know."

Cup of freshly poured coffee in her hand, Sam turned abruptly. The hot liquid sloshed out of the cup and landed right on target—Adam's fly.

He shouted a curse and stepped back.

"Oh, I'm *so* sorry!" she cried in mock alarm. "I couldn't hear what you'd said and I wanted you to repeat it." Loud enough for your brother and your wife to hear, she thought with a taste of revenge. "How clumsy of me."

At that moment she knew that if Adam could have gotten his hands around her throat, her life wouldn't have been worth a plugged nickel. His face had turned beet red; a vein pulsed at his temple.

In contrast, Eileen's face had gone ghostly pale.

Beside her, a laugh rumbled up from Rogan's chest and his hand slid across her shoulders in a welcome caress. "I should have warned you, big brother. *Nobody* messes with Sam. She's one tough lady."

Strangely enough, that sounded like a compliment, and Sam basked in the warm glow of Rogan's praise throughout the rest of the day.

That evening, as they were taking their customary walk along the beach, she confessed, "I don't much like your brother."

"Some days I don't, either."

They walked side by side, their strides matched in a rhythm synchronized with the sea. Muted waves spilled over themselves, traveling lazily toward the shore. An arcing line of shimmering foam marked their retreat in the moon glow. A cool breeze whispered through the air, teasing at her curls and sending gooseflesh down her bare arms.

To Sam's surprise, Rogan caught her hand and stopped her. Her heart skidded to a halt, then picked up at a faster beat.

He never touched her on these walks. He always kept just out of reach, as if he was afraid of even the suggestion of intimacy. All he'd offered was companionship. Until now.

Turning, she looked up into his shadowed face. She couldn't read his expression. But she sensed his desire in the way his fingers folded around hers, in the rapid rise and fall of his chest.

Hallelujah! He wasn't entirely immune to her after all.

"I'd like you to stay away from Adam."

"I have every intention of doing just that."

He wove his fingers through hers. "When he decides to use his money, women tend to find him very persuasive."

"I wouldn't." The very thought of being seduced by big brother Adam gave her the willies. Because of her foolish heart, Rogan was a whole different story.

With his free hand, he traced a line along her jaw. "There's something very stubborn about you, Samantha Sterling."

"It's one of my finest attributes."

"Yes, I think that's true." His head dipped toward hers.

Sam waited in breathless anticipation.

The stars haloed Rogan's head, a fiery aurora that made Sam think of power and ancient gods come to conquer those who were mere mortals. A fanciful thought but one that seemed appropriate in an instinctive, deeply feminine way.

He filled her view as he inched closer. His hand slid around the back of her neck, threading his fingers through her hair and capturing her. She didn't want to escape.

Protesting his slow progress, she made a low, throaty sound of frustration. To hell with waiting, she thought wildly. She'd kiss him!

Their lips fused and she didn't know whether she or Rogan had closed the final minuscule gap between them. She only knew that it was his heat she wanted, his taste she craved.

She swayed into his embrace. He pulled her closer. They were both wearing shorts and his hair-roughened thighs brushed against hers, the friction sending sparks of desire racing to her midsection. As their tongues courted in an ancient ritual, their bodies sought a match of hard against soft. An ache grew deep inside her.

He cupped her buttocks and tugged her into the nest of his hips. She nearly shattered at the feel of the hard ridge he pressed between her thighs.

His groan of response vibrated through her whole body.

She was going to come apart. Here on a public beach, albeit a dark one. She'd never done anything like that. Had never felt so wanton.

Apparently he sensed how close they were to going over the edge.

With a jagged breath, he retreated. He gripped her by the shoulders. "Ah, Carrot Top…"

Together they stood on the beach, breathing hard, their bodies locked like two gladiators who had just done battle and were now willing to accept a draw.

"That's something else I've got to tell you," he said. His words rasped through his throat with each ragged breath he drew.

Sam's heart slammed against her ribs. "What's that?"

"When I fix you up with a guy, hold back on the first kiss. You don't want to give him too much all at once."

The chill air coated her in gooseflesh. Hold back? She could no more have resisted Rogan's kiss, or subdued her response, than she could have resisted a tidal wave.

"I'll keep that in mind," she managed to say as she forced her stubborn chin up a notch.

"Other guys might not be able to restrain themselves."

"But you have exceptional willpower."

"I used to think so."

Sam's jaw began to ache, her own restraint reaching record highs. "Rogan, I ought to clobber you. First you tell me I'm too athletic. Then you want me to act like a bimbo. Now you're saying I can't kiss worth beans." Her fists clenched in frustration. "I've had it with you. I'm outta here."

Whirling, she marched up the beach toward Rogan's house.

He stood like a statue watching her go. He'd blown it. Big-time.

Couldn't she tell how much her strength and intelligence appealed to him? And her kiss? Damn, he didn't want her kissing any other man like that. Ever!

In every way he could think of, Samantha Sterling knocked his socks off.

And that was dangerous. More for her than it was for him.

Forcing one foot in front of the other, he followed her back to the house. How could he explain how he felt? How she affected him?

And did he dare tell her the truth?

When he got inside the phone was ringing. Without giving much thought to who might be calling, he picked up the receiver.

HAPHAZARDLY, Sam stuffed her clothes into the suitcase, slammed it shut and headed downstairs. To hell with Garcia and her performance reviews. She wasn't going to stay here another minute.

And she damn well wasn't going to cry over Rogan Prescott.

She arrived at the foot of the stairs just as Rogan hung up the phone.

"My sister-in-law has been arrested."

Sam came to an abrupt halt. "Eileen?" she clarified.

"Right. I'm going downtown to see if I can get her out."

Dropping her suitcase where she stood, she said, "I'm coming with you."

He eyed her speculatively. "Okay, let's go."

"What was Eileen arrested for?" Sam asked minutes later as she snapped her seat belt in place.

Shifting into reverse, he whipped the Bronco into traffic. Horns blared and tires squealed as passing cars tried to avoid a collision.

"I'm not entirely sure. She was pretty hysterical."

"Eileen called you instead of her husband?"

"Adam isn't always the picture of patience and understanding. I guess she thought I wouldn't go ballistic on her."

"Smart girl," Sam mumbled. She would have doubted Eileen would even violate traffic laws, much less do something that would result in her arrest. Perhaps it was all a mistake. The police had been known to make errors.

"Some detective named Garcia came on the line. Said I was to ask for him."

Her eyes widened. If Garcia was involved, chances were good Eileen's arrest had something to do with the jewelry thefts. It was hard to believe a reticent young woman like Eileen, who appeared thoroughly cowered by her domineering husband, was the brains behind the string of thefts that had rocked the social set for months now. Something didn't add up. Unless she was just the mule acting under the direction of someone else.

In spite of heavy evening traffic, they reached the West L.A. police station in record time.

At the front door, they met two detectives who were leaving. One of them recognized Sam and eyed her tight-fitting jeans appreciatively.

"Hi, doll, how's it—"

With a silencing shake of her head, she hurried past them, wishing she had taken time to change into a more professional outfit instead of casual clothes for her drive home. She was going to have to walk a tightrope here at the station not to give herself away—or have some other officer inadvertently reveal her identity to Rogan.

But then, with Eileen under arrest, maybe the case had been solved and her undercover assignment would be over.

She should have been pleased at the prospect.

Perversely, she wasn't.

# Chapter Six

"We nabbed her at a pawnshop in Santa Monica just before closing time. The owner called it in, kept her talking till we could get there, and we caught her red-handed."

Arms folded, Detective Garcia had his butt propped on the edge of his desk in the squad room. Sam thought he looked darn proud of himself. She couldn't tell what Rogan was thinking, but he did look troubled. They hadn't been allowed to see Eileen yet. Instead, after being logged in as "visitors" at the front desk—to maintain Sam's undercover status—they'd been told to sit and pay homage to Garcia.

"You're telling me that my sister-in-law stole her own necklace?"

"Now listen up, Prescott. Your brother has been making a big stink about finding the thief but I notice he was damn quick to file an insurance claim. Either his wife snatched the necklace for a little pocket money, or we're talking insurance fraud and your brother's in on it up to his ears."

"There'd be no reason for Adam to make a fraudulent claim. My brother has plenty of money."

Sam said, "When we saw him yesterday, he was very upset about the theft. I don't think he was acting."

Garcia shot her a dismissive look. "Everybody can get into a bind. Maybe the cards don't fall right one too many times in a friendly little game of high-stakes poker. Or he's got a lady on the side who wants an extra trinket." He lifted his shoulders as if it didn't matter to him as long as he made the collar. "You tell me, Mr. Prescott. What was your sister-in-law up to?"

"What did she tell you?"

"Nothing. Said she wouldn't talk until she saw you first."

"Good for her." Looking grim, Rogan stood. Even though he was still wearing cutoffs and a tatty gray sweatshirt with the sleeves ripped off, he carried himself with so much authority, Garcia rose in response. "I'd like to see Eileen now."

"Keep in mind we've got a whole rash of jewel thefts on our hands. Your sister-in-law just moved to the top of the suspect list."

"Ridiculous." Rogan scoffed at the possibility. Eileen wasn't the kind of person who'd go around lifting necklaces off of unwary women. She was too anxious to please people, including her husband. Something else was going on and Rogan was determined to find out what it was.

"Ms. Sterling can wait here for you," the detective said.

Rogan sent Sam a questioning look.

"You go ahead," she said. "Eileen will probably

be more comfortable talking to you alone than if I tag along. We don't exactly know each other real well.''

"She may need a woman's shoulder to cry on.''

A soft, sexy smile curled Sam's lips. "Most women I know would chose a man's shoulder over a woman's any day of the week. You'll do just fine. I'll be here if you need me.''

Rogan thought about that for a minute, then nodded. At least Sam wasn't planning to duck out. She'd be there for backup if he needed her.

The detective led him down a drab hallway that had all the pizzazz of a last walk to the electric chair and let him in to what Rogan assumed was an interrogation room. Eileen sat hunched over a scarred-looking table, her hands folded together so tightly her knuckles were white.

When she looked up, her chin started to wobble and tears spilled down her cheeks.

She looked so darn forlorn, she reminded Rogan of a lost puppy who'd been badly abused. He figured he was the one who would have to rescue her.

GARCIA RETURNED from delivering Rogan to the interrogation room and plopped down in the swivel chair behind his desk. "You're looking very fetching, *Officer* Sterling.''

Straightening, Sam returned her superior's gaze levelly. "I'm on an undercover assignment, as you may recall, sir. Jeans are appropriate attire for people who live at the beach.''

"It's not often one of L.A.'s finest gets her photo in a national tabloid.''

Her eyes widened. "What photo?''

"You made the big time at that charity shindig you attended with Rogan. The beautiful people at play."

"I didn't know." Though she did vaguely recall flashbulbs popping. Evidently getting a picture in the paper was such an ordinary occurrence for Rogan, no one had bothered to mention it.

Garcia tipped back in his chair, tenting his fingers in front of his narrow lips. "So what have you learned about Prescott while you've been enjoying the good life?"

*That Rogan's kisses set her off like a Fourth of July sky rocket.* "I don't believe Rogan Prescott is involved in the jewel thefts."

"What about his associates and members of the family?"

"I've found no evidence that any of them is linked to the thefts."

"Except they've been at the parties when the thief strikes."

"True," she conceded. But that didn't mean Rogan was a crook. In fact, she sensed he was too generous by far to steal anything.

Garcia studied her in silence for such a long time, Sam fought the urge to squirm under his intense scrutiny. "What connection do any of these people have to Florida?" he asked.

"Florida?" she echoed, caught off guard by his unexpected question.

He nodded. "I was going through some old Wanted notices and came across a series of jewelry thefts that happened two and three years ago in Florida. The M.O. was pretty close to the same as what's going on around here."

Searching through her memory, Sam came up with a couple of thoughts that gave her pause. "That first night at Geoffrey Hughes's house, Rogan mentioned he was hiding out upstairs from a woman from Florida." A woman who was bent on marriage, Sam recalled. Presumably to Rogan. "It could be he knew her there. And his aunt Agatha evidently has friends in Florida who contribute to her charity causes. She mentioned that this morning."

"See if you can find out when Rogan and his aunt were there. If the dates coincide with these other thefts…"

He left the thought unfinished, which made Sam squirm. Someone in the Prescott family could indeed be the Westside jewel thief.

"I gather you've decided Eileen isn't the culprit?" she asked.

"Not necessarily. She could be guilty. Or she could be nothing more than an inept copycat who tried to take advantage of the situation. Either way, she may know something that'll help us out."

Detective Garcia was obviously holding his cards close to his vest. Sam could hardly argue with that. But it did mean she wouldn't be able to walk out on Rogan so easily, not if her boss needed information about a Florida connection.

She sighed. *This* time she'd have to make darn sure she kept her distance from Rogan. Absolutely—*positively*—no more kisses allowed. Not that Rogan had given her a gold star for the one they'd shared earlier that evening. He didn't like the way she'd reacted. But then, neither did she. She'd nearly lost herself in that kiss right there on a public beach.

And with no effort at all, she could still recall his taste, his sweet flavor and the press of his lips against hers, the way his tongue had...

WHEN ROGAN RETURNED to the squad room, his dark eyebrows were pulled into a grim line and evening whiskers shadowed the stern set of his jaw.

"I've called an attorney friend of mine," he told Sam, who had hung around long after Garcia had wandered off. The whole building felt empty, at least the second floor had as she'd paced impatiently. "He says it'll take him a half hour or so before he can get here. Let's get some coffee."

"There's a machine in the break room. One of the officers told me," she quickly added, realizing that was a bit of knowledge she might not be expected to have as a visitor to the police station. "Probably not gourmet."

"It'll do."

The door to the break room stood open, the air inside slightly fetid from too many bodies that had spent the day sipping coffee and bragging about conquests, both romantic and in the law enforcement arena. The constant macho conversation among the officers was one of those things Sam had tried to overlook since she'd joined the force, but it still made her feel uncomfortable.

For now, however, the room was empty and eerily quiet except for the ticking clock above the corkboard covered with announcements.

Her breath caught. The newspaper photo of her and Rogan was thumbtacked to the board right next to promotional opportunities. Damn, every guy in the station was going to razz her for that. A small, irritating voice in her head reminded Sam how much she hated being teased. *You're too soft,* it taunted, reminding her cops of either gender had to wear a tough shell that she still hadn't quite mastered.

Sam sidled toward the bulletin board while Rogan headed directly for the coffee machine. It wouldn't do for him to spot the photo and ask too many questions.

She snatched the clipping and stuffed it into her purse. Rogan was so distracted he hadn't noticed her detour.

She joined him at the coffee machine, holding her own questions until he had dropped several quarters into the machine and extracted two coffees—one with extra sugar for him.

Then she asked, "What did you find out from Eileen?"

"That my brother is a worse jerk than I had thought."

"He's the perp?" she blurted. Immediately she wished she could snag the words back. She tried to cover herself by saying, "She said Adam stole the necklace?"

Rogan didn't seem to notice her verbal slip into police jargon. It was growing increasingly difficult, particularly here at the police station, to maintain the charade of an idle socialite when Sam normally worked at being one of the guys, a hard-edged cop. Neither role appeared to sit too comfortably on her shoulders, she mused, trying not to consider what that could mean for her future on the force—or with Rogan.

Pulling a metal folding chair away from the table,

he straddled it and sat. "No, the Prescott specialty is breaking a woman's heart, not stealing."

"What do you mean?"

"I knew Adam was fooling around. That's not news. He's always had a woman or two on the side. Being a first-class carouser is an old family tradition, probably started by my great-grandfather. But I didn't know Eileen knew. Understandably, she wants out of the marriage. But Adam keeps her on a very tight leash, hardly enough petty cash to take a bus out of town. And she was foolish enough when they got married to sign a prenuptial agreement. According to an attorney she consulted on the sly, it would leave her practically penniless if she asked for a divorce."

Feeling suddenly chilled, Sam sank onto a chair across the table from Rogan. She wrapped her fingers around her cup of coffee but her sense of dread went more than surface deep. "The courts would let that happen?"

He shrugged. "The Prescotts retain some very sharp lawyers. The agreement would stand up in court long enough to make Eileen's life miserable and financially break any attorney who tried to fight for her rights."

"Then she did steal the necklace," Sam concluded, recognizing the act as one of desperation for a woman who had no other source of cash.

"If you can say she stole something that already belonged to her. She figured she'd pawn it and use the money to start over again. I don't think she realized how little on the dollar she'd get for it. Not much of a nest egg after six years of putting up with my brother."

"At least she won't be charged with grand theft."

"I don't know. Detective Garcia seems determined to make some kind of a case out of it. Insurance fraud, if nothing else." His fingers worked restlessly through his hair, creating chaos rather than smoothing the dark strands. "That's why I called my attorney friend."

"Even if he can get Eileen released, where will she go? Surely she doesn't want to go back home, not if Adam finds out what she's done."

"For now we'll take her back to my place. She can either stay with me, or with Aunt Agatha, if she'd rather." He lifted his shoulders in a worried shrug. "Then I'm going to have a long talk with my brother."

Sam's chest filled with an emotion she didn't dare name. She'd seen too much of the Prescott family and all their peccadilloes, and been hurt too deeply as a child by her own father's desertion, to trust a man easily. But Rogan's gesture of caring touched her deeply, weakening the barricade she'd so carefully built around her heart.

She slid her hand across the table to cover his. "Bringing home another stray, are you?"

His wry smile didn't quite vanquish the bleakness from his deep blue eyes. He squeezed her fingers. "Somebody's got to do the right thing."

"So you're elected."

"Yeah, and when we find you a guy to marry I'm going to make damn sure there's no prenuptial agreement to screw you up. You can count on it, Carrot Top."

If he had struck her in the chest with a spiked volleyball, the wind couldn't have been driven from her lungs more completely. He was still set on marrying her off to someone else—*to rescue her,* dammit!

She stood so quickly the chair she'd been sitting on fell over backward, crashing to the floor. "I really appreciate your concern, Rogan." She spat out the words. "But I think I can find my own husband, *if* and when I decide I even want one. Which, at this point, is likely to be in the middle of the next century."

"And after I get Eileen settled," he continued, staring at his coffee cup as if he hadn't heard a word Sam had said, "you and I are going up to Bakersfield. We're going to ask a few questions of our own at that jewelry store where Garcia said some of the stolen jewels turned up. These thefts are affecting my family now and they've got to stop."

Dumbfounded, she looked at him. In spite of being a trained police officer, her emotions roiled like a volcano about to erupt. She knew she ought to be happy to race out to Bakersfield to pursue this case. But she wasn't. She wanted Rogan to...to...

Dear heaven, she didn't know what she wanted Rogan to do, but the surge of adrenaline she felt told her to flee. For her life, if nothing else. Certainly to protect her heart.

"You're out of your mind, Prescott. I'm not going anywhere with you." How the hell could he just ignore her statement about marriage as if her hot words hadn't been spoken? Didn't he care?

Whirling, she marched out of the break room and stormed into the squad room. She all but ran right smack into Garcia.

"That man's a lunatic!" she complained. "He wants me to—" She swallowed the words "marry someone else" before they escaped her lips. "He wants me to go with him to Bakersfield to investigate the jewel thefts. He wants to ask his own damn questions. Of all the nerve, the absolute gall. Does he think he's a vigilante or something? Of all the—"

"Sounds like a good idea to me," Garcia drawled. The corners of his lips twitched, almost as if he'd considered smiling but had dismissed the idea as a waste of energy.

Her mouth dropped open. "He's a civilian, for heaven's sake. What can he find out that the local police haven't—"

"Who knows? These rich suckers have their own ways of getting answers. Go with him and find out what you can. At this point, we haven't got much to lose."

Not much to lose? How about her sanity?

She did not—absolutely *not*—want to go anywhere with Rogan Prescott.

Garcia's eyes narrowed. "Have a nice trip, *Officer* Sterling. Check in with me when you get back. Meanwhile, I'll be working on your performance review. Success on an undercover assignment can be a real plum when you're looking for advancement."

Garcia's implied threat did not escape Sam's notice, and she bristled—not for the first time—at the compromises she'd had to make to turn herself into a peg that would fit the mold that L.A.P.D. demanded of her.

IT WAS AFTER MIDNIGHT before Eileen was finally released into Rogan's custody. She was visibly shivering as she climbed into the front seat of the Bronco.

Silently cursing his brother, Rogan yanked an old sweatshirt from the back of the vehicle and handed it to his sister-in-law.

"I'm sorry," she whispered.

"Quit apologizing," he said more gruffly than he'd intended. "None of this is your fault." Adam was to blame for the desperation that had driven his wife to hock a few jewels. *Chock up another victim on the Prescott scorecard,* he thought bitterly, remembering his mother and how much his father had hurt her by his philandering. And the damage he himself had done to a young woman who'd deserved better.

From the back seat, Sam leaned forward to rest a reassuring hand on Eileen's shoulder. "Don't worry. Rogan's into rescuing damsels in distress."

"But you've been living with him," she protested. "I mean, I don't want to be in the way, if you and Rogan—"

"Trust me, Eileen, you won't be in the way," Sam insisted.

Rogan started the truck and backed out of the parking space. "I've got lots of bedrooms. Having you there won't be any problem at all."

"I don't even have a toothbrush, or anything to sleep in." The tremble in her voice matched the wobble of her chin.

Sam met Rogan's eyes in the rearview mirror, and her heart squeezed tight. "That's okay," she said. "He's a virtual Boy Scout—always prepared."

"I won't stay long. I promise."

On some level, Sam hoped Eileen would hang

around for quite a while—at least until the case was closed. Having her in the house would provide a buffer between Sam and Rogan, and with any luck she'd be able to keep her yo-yoing emotions in check. Right now she was vacillating between hating Rogan for the way he was so determined to marry her off to some other man—and loving him because he could care so much about Eileen's mistreatment by his brother.

Life was decidedly unfair.

CALIFORNIA POPPIES were still blooming at the higher elevations along Gorman Pass on the way to Bakersfield.

Sam was still nurturing her anger, like a seed that was on the verge of sprouting but had been thwarted by the lack of enough sun.

It had been three days since Rogan had royally ticked her off. She'd hardly spoken to him since. It hadn't appeared to matter. He'd been fully engrossed in dealing with Eileen and her problems, an absorption that Sam would have found admirable if she hadn't been so darn mad.

How could a man who was so basically good and caring be so incredibly dense? It made her blood boil.

And it didn't help that he looked like some Hollywood cowboy today with a silk Western-cut shirt, tight-fitting jeans and expensive, hand-tooled boots. Resting his arm casually on the open window, the wind caught the walnut strands of his hair and tossed them about like an eager lover.

"So tell me, Rogan," she said, easing back into the rich upholstery of the Bronco and trying to relax the tight clamp of her jaw. "Have you spent much time in Florida?"

He slid her an easy smile. "Aunt Agatha used to have a condo in Miami so she could hang around with some of her cronies from New York. I'd go down there a couple of times a year to sail the Keys with a buddy."

Perversely, she wanted to ask if his "buddy" had been male or female. "When was the last time you were there?"

Going far faster than the speed limit, Rogan shot past an eighteen-wheeler hugging the right lane. Sam hoped he wouldn't get a ticket. Garcia would love to hang that around her neck like a persistent clove of garlic.

"It's been a couple of years," Rogan answered. "In spite of appearances, Agatha is slowing down a little. Cross-country travel is getting to be too much for her. And the charities she loves best are right here in L.A."

"But she still gets contributions from her friends in Florida?"

"I suppose. If she asks, it's really hard to say no, even if you're living three thousand miles away from her."

In spite of herself, Sam smiled. She'd sent her check to Chandler House a week ago, though the amount was probably less than what Rogan carried in his wallet on a daily basis. For her, the contribution had been substantial. She hoped Aunt Agatha understood that.

Oddly, she wondered if Rogan had inherited some

charitable gene from his aunt, a gene that had mutated into rescuing stray dogs and helpless women.

Darn it all! she thought as she stared out the window, the splashes of late spring color—yellow, orange and purple—bright against the green hillsides. Sam wasn't helpless, and she didn't want any man to see her that way. That was how her mother had been. Sam had hated that.

When they reached the outskirts of Bakersfield, Rogan pulled off the highway to get gas. The weekday business was light and he pulled up to an otherwise deserted row of pumps. A single car was parked at the curb in front of the minimart, an old Oldsmobile that sat low on its springs.

Sam got out of the Bronco when Rogan did and he took the opportunity to admire her as she stretched and rolled her shoulders, relaxing after the two-hour ride. One fine-looking woman, he thought. It was a real shame he'd vowed she was off-limits to him. But it was better for her that way. The mess Adam had made of Eileen's life was a good reminder that Prescott men didn't make suitable husbands.

Still, he couldn't help but appreciate the way Sam's rust-colored blouse set off her hair and how her long legs looked even longer thanks to the cut of her tailored slacks.

"You want a snack or anything while I'm inside?" Sam asked, obviously planning a trip to the ladies' room.

"No, that's okay. We'll catch lunch in Bakersfield."

"Fine. I'll just be a minute."

Keeping one eye on the pleasant sway of her hips

as she walked away, he pulled out his wallet and found his bank card. He had just slid it into the Automated Teller Machine when all hell broke loose.

Gunfire exploded inside the minimart.

Somebody screamed.

A man in a pea cap and dark jacket came barreling out the door, gun in hand.

Rogan was about to shout a warning to Sam when he saw her launch herself at the gunman. They hit the ground together, the man bellowing his surprise.

Before Rogan could get his feet out of the mental concrete that gripped him, Sam had subdued the would-be robber and had him flat on his face, one arm in a hammerlock, and her own weapon sticking in the guy's ear.

He hadn't known she was carrying her piece, much less seen her draw it from her purse.

"My God…" Rogan murmured. He'd never seen anyone move that fast. Certainly not a woman. Didn't Sam realize she could have gotten herself killed?

"Rogan!" Sam shouted. "Get inside and have someone call 9-1-1. Check to see if anyone is hurt."

Her order released his paralysis.

He raced inside, skirting Sam and her prisoner. "You okay?" he asked.

"I've got everything under control here. Just make that call."

Inside, Rogan found a shaken but uninjured woman behind the counter. She'd already called the police and as he was still trying to get his bearings, the wail of sirens penetrated the sound of her sobs. She looked to be okay, though, so Rogan went back to see how Sam was doing. When he'd seen her take down the robber, his stomach had turned to knots. He could still hardly draw a decent breath.

There'd never been another time in his life when he'd been so scared—not for himself, but for Sam.

God, he didn't want anything bad to happen to her.

He found her talking to one of the cops while another couple of uniformed officers had the holdup man spread-eagled against the hood of their black-and-white.

Fear turned to anger, and the temper he normally considered mild shifted to a boiling rage. He tried to get a grip on himself...and failed.

Rogan walked up to Sam and shouted, "What kind of a crazy stunt was that?" His heart was pumping a million miles an hour with the aftereffects of a massive surge of adrenaline. "Don't you know you could have been killed?" She looked so damn calm, he almost throttled her himself right there in front of half the Bakersfield police force.

She slipped her arm around his waist and led him away from the officer she'd been talking to. "Easy, Rogan, it's all over now."

"Don't *easy* me. What if you'd been—"

"I knew what I was doing, Rogan. It's okay."

"How did you know? The guy was twice your size—"

"I've had training, and surprise was on my side."

"My God, a couple of classes in judo and you thought you could take a man down—"

To Rogan's surprise, Sam wrapped her arms around him and hugged him. Hard. That made him feel a little better. She was a strong woman. Substantial. He breathed a little easier.

"You pull a stunt like that again," he warned, nuzzling his face against her soft, sweet-smelling curls, "and I'm likely to shoot you myself."

Her light laughter spiraled through his midsection, untangling one kind of knot and tightening others in an arousing battle of push-me, pull-you. He leaned back enough so he could cup her face between his hands and look into her gorgeous green eyes. Then he kissed her. Right there at a gas station on the outskirts of Bakersfield in front of a dozen cops.

She tasted so damn good, nothing else mattered.

Later he'd remind himself how she was off-limits to him. Much later. And then maybe he'd worry about how Sam could wrestle a guy to the ground without even getting her clothes wrinkled.

But not now.

Now he took the time to savor her uniqueness. Her fingers flexed into his shirt, like a kitten, and he heard her purr a low, throaty sound as his tongue toyed with hers. Threading his fingers through her tousled curls and massaging her scalp, he changed the angle of the kiss, dipping more deeply into her flavor.

Vaguely he became aware of voices around them, the shove of Sam's palms against his chest. With great reluctance, he broke the kiss.

"Don't ever do that again," he said in a low growl.

High color rode on her cheeks and her eyes were as dark green as a forest. "I had no intention of kissing you this time," she said with a snap. "You were the one who—"

"Not that," he corrected. "Don't be a hero, Sam. It's too damn hard on my heart."

Sam allowed a small smile to curl her lips. How

on earth was she supposed to deal with a man who set her on fire one minute with a kiss, then either ignored her or persisted in trying to marry her off to someone else the next? The guy was driving her nuts.

FLIPPING OPEN his wallet, Rogan waved it in the general direction of the Bakersfield jewelry store owner. "L.A.P.D. We've got some questions we'd like to ask you."

Sam rolled her eyes. Now Rogan was impersonating an officer, and she was an accomplice. If Garcia heard about this, she'd likely be facing suspension even if it had been his idea she toddle along with Rogan to investigate the case.

"I've already spoken with our local police," the owner responded. His frizzy gray hair looked like an oversize Brillo pad and he had a matching goatee. The store was decidedly upscale with plush carpeting, well-lighted display cases, and a discreet sign in the front window reading Jewelry Purchased.

"Then you won't mind answering our questions," Rogan said. "Naturally, we have a reciprocal agreement between our two fine cities."

*Naturally?* Rogan didn't have a clue about police agency turf wars. But, what the heck? She might as well go along since her neck was out about a mile anyway. Her heart was none too secure at the moment, either, not since Rogan had kissed her at the gas station. Lord, no man ought to be able to turn a woman's legs to rubber with a single kiss.

Well, given the duration of that particular kiss, maybe it was the equivalent of two or three performed by any ordinary man. Rogan might not be able to paint pictures but he could sure coax a powerful emotional response from a woman. It had been more than an hour since he'd kissed her and she was still trembling inside. *And,* darn it all, wanting more.

Even the police interrogation regarding the holdup at the minimart hadn't dimmed her memory of Rogan's lips caressing hers, his tongue fencing intimately as she parried in response.

She had to forcefully drag her thoughts back to the present to listen to the store owner describe the man who had pawned the emeralds.

"He was probably six feet, slender build, and definitely had a British accent."

That description certainly fit Geoffrey Hughes, but he'd be only one of hundreds. "How old was he?" she asked.

"Mature, is my recollection. Perhaps fifty. Maybe older."

She frowned. "Did you tell that to the police who interviewed you?"

"I don't recall if they asked."

If not, it certainly would have been a major oversight that left the L.A.P.D. still thinking the perp might be Geoffrey. There was no way he could be mistaken for a man over fifty unless he'd been wearing makeup. She supposed, at this point, anything was possible.

Rogan asked, "Was he alone?"

"He came into the store by himself but I had the impression there was someone else in the vehicle with him. Probably a woman." The front door opened and two well-dressed women entered. The owner's gaze slid in their direction and he smiled. "I only know the gentleman arrived in a limousine, accepted cash for the emerald necklace and left. Later I discovered, to my regret, that the jewels were stolen property. Now, you really must excuse me.''

Dismissing them with a nod, the owner left them standing at the counter display case filled with fine jewelry and went to tend to his customers. Diamonds, emeralds and perfectly matched strands of pearls glistened in the soft light against a background of royal blue.

''See anything you like?'' Rogan asked.

In spite of herself, Sam's attention strayed to an exquisite emerald pendant with matching earrings. ''Even without seeing the price tags—which are neatly hidden, I notice—I know there's not a thing in this store that fits my budget.''

He gazed thoughtfully at the display. ''Someday you'll have the very best. I'll see to it, Carrot Top.''

# Chapter Seven

"He's the very *best* you could find?"

Planting her fists on her hips, Sam glared at Rogan. The setting sun over the Pacific glowed through the sliding glass doors of his house, haloing him like an Adonis rising from the sea.

Goofus padded across the room and parked himself at Sam's feet. Looking up hopefully, he whined.

Ignoring the dog, Sam gritted her teeth. A sea *serpent* was closer to the truth when it came to Rogan Prescott! A slimy green snake slithering through the—

"Eileen and Aunt Agatha suggested him. Theo Emmanoulides is worth megabucks. And he's a very nice man."

"I've met him. He was at Geoffrey's party. He's an *old* man, for heaven's sake."

"Not so old. Maybe fifty."

"He was that old when I was born," she wailed. Rogan hadn't been paying one whit of attention to her since they'd returned from Bakersfield yesterday. Instead he'd been closeted with Eileen, evidently planning this sham of a blind date. Sam had thought

Eileen was her *friend!* No way! Not if she conspired to recommend Theo. "I can't believe you've fixed me up on a blind date with a candidate for the geriatric ward."

"You'll have a good time. He always goes first-class."

Her eyes narrowed when he deliberately avoided her gaze. "All right." She yanked off the sweatshirt she'd been wearing to cover her swim suit during her evening walk along the beach and fisted it in her hand. Her frustration with her job, herself—*and* Rogan—made her reckless. "What time is he picking me up?"

"He said eight o'clock. That doesn't give you much time to get ready."

"No problem." She ground her teeth together. No job was worth this much grief. She'd make that perfectly clear to Garcia first thing Monday morning. "I can hardly wait."

Picking up a velvet box from the breakfast bar, Rogan held it out to her. "I thought these would look really nice with that green dress you were wearing at Geoffrey's house. Theo knows quality when he sees it."

She snatched it from his hand. "I'm not starring in *My Fair Lady*, Rogan, and you're not Professor What's-his-name. You don't have to tell me what to wear. I know—" When she lifted the lid on the box, the earth stood still.

A solitary emerald pendant, the stone the size of a robin's egg, gazed back at her from a bed of satin, the gem attached to a white-gold chain that by itself had to be worth a fortune. Above the necklace rested matching earrings, a perfect set of green teardrops—the set she'd seen, admired and secretly coveted in Bakersfield.

He'd noticed, damn him! And with a thoughtfulness, not to mention a budget, that was rare in men, had bought them for her. They must have arrived by special messenger while she was out.

Her throat closed around the tears she wanted to shed—for Rogan, for her, for the futility of her even dreaming of a long-term relationship with a playboy millionaire. A Prescott. "Oh, Rogan, I can't accept these. They're too—"

"They'll be stunning. Let me show you."

Taking the necklace from the box, he turned her around. His experienced fingers worked with gentle dexterity as he slid the necklace around her throat, the weight of the stone heavy against her breastbone, and latched it at the nape of her neck. His warm breath was a sweet, heated caress across her bare skin, the touch of his hands a tender stroke that sent an ache of wanting radiating toward her midsection.

The man was impossible. Generous beyond reason. So blind he couldn't see how she felt about him—not that she was entirely sure herself. The value of the emeralds meant nothing to her. His thoughtfulness did. But he didn't appear to care a fig about her.

He turned her so she could admire his gift in the distorted reflection of the chrome toaster on the breakfast bar. "I suppose you could say the necklace is a bit much to go with a swimsuit, but you get the idea."

The image blurred before her eyes. His hands were resting on her shoulders, almost lovingly. The wry tilt of his lips suggested both tenderness and caring.

Slowly, his head dipped toward her shoulder. The brush of his lips at the juncture of her neck and shoulder was so light it was more illusion than reality. Even so, it sent a curl of heat flooding through her body. An aching need filled her chest and tightened in her throat.

Rotating away from their dual image, she looked up into his brilliant blue eyes and found they had deepened to nearly black. With trembling fingers, she brushed back a stray lock of dark hair from his forehead. Her heart thudded heavily against her ribs, almost painfully, as she waited and wanted and held her breath.

Dammit all! She knew Rogan wanted her whether he was willing to admit it or not. And she'd had about all the masquerading she could stand. Somehow, at that moment, it didn't matter that hundreds of women eagerly pursued Rogan. Right now, this minute, she wanted him for herself.

"Go on, Carrot Top." The raspy sound of his voice cut across her heart, slicing her with his rejection. "Theo's gonna love you. He won't be able to resist."

Taking her hand from his face, he placed the velvet box in her palm.

Sam didn't cry. She didn't scream or go running out of the house, slamming the door behind her—though she considered all of that and more.

Instead she simply turned and went upstairs. She'd pack, move back to her duplex and tell Garcia if this is what it meant to be a cop, she didn't want any part of it. It was one thing to put her life on the line to catch a crook; it was something quite different to risk her heart. And the glorified goal of being a police officer, of preventing tragic murders like those that had taken the lives of her friends, had dimmed considerably of late.

But, dear God, she could still hear Dee's infectious laughter, which would start off sounding like a cackling hen laying an egg and end with a snort. And somewhere in the back of Sam's closet she still had the sweater Marcia had knit for her the Christmas of their sophomore year. One arm had been a good four inches shorter than the other one because Marcia hadn't had enough time to finish the job. That small flaw, and all the love that had gone into the making of the sweater, had made Sam cherish the gift all the more—though she'd never actually had the nerve to wear it.

But maybe, in spite of all that, Sam needed to take another look at her own life—and what it meant to be a cop.

Indeed it might be time for her to take another look at her life.

ROGAN WATCHED Sam mount the stairs with quiet dignity, Goofus following her in a blatant act of betrayal and disloyalty.

Sam's back was straight, her long legs beautifully sculpted and tanned like those of a first-rate model. It didn't take fancy clothes or jewelry to make her a class act. Whatever she wore, Sam was one special lady.

Which was why it had been so hard for him to come up with a man worthy of her. Even Theo had seemed not quite good enough, although Eileen had convinced him to give him a chance. Of a poor batch of prospects—drawn from virtually the entire L.A. social register—he was the best.

That didn't mean Rogan liked the idea of Sam actually going out with the guy. The thought of her hanging on Theo's every word held little appeal. Even less, the possibility that he might hold her hand. Or, Lord help him, kiss her good-night. Beyond that, Rogan couldn't even contemplate the possibilities. It made him too sick to his stomach.

The only other choice would be for Rogan to step into the breach to give her the wealth and status she apparently desired. But he couldn't do that. She was a woman who deserved far better than a Prescott.

Hadn't his brother's recent antics proved that once again? Rogan was determined not to make the same mistake. He didn't want to cause Sam the same heartbreak his mother and Eileen had experienced.

After all, an ersatz big brother was supposed to protect his little sister.

Too bad he hadn't realized how much it would hurt.

"GOOFUS, can't you stay out from under foot?" Sam's voice wobbled, the words catching in her throat as she nearly stumbled against the chest of drawers. With trembling fingers, she removed the emerald necklace and placed it back in its box.

Pushing the dog out of her way, she tugged her suitcase from the back of the closet and slammed it down on top of the bed. The strap snagged on itself. She yanked it free, breaking a fingernail in the process.

"Oh, double damn!" she muttered. Her vision

blurred as she gnawed on the broken nail. She was *not* going to let Rogan Prescott get to her.

Goofus dropped to the floor and put his paws over his nose. His ridiculous tail swept a clean arc back and forth as he eyed Sam.

"Are you all right?" Eileen stepped into the room. Recovered from her ordeal at the police station and growing emotionally stronger every day, she looked stunning. Her mascara never seemed to smudge, her vermilion lipstick never smeared, and her long blond hair glistened with such a high sheen that shampoo companies should have been breaking down the door to hire her for their commercials.

In contrast, Sam's hair was more like a clown's wig and her freckles were impossible to hide no matter how much makeup she wore. With a sigh, Sam forcefully tamped down a stab of envy. Eileen had her own set of problems to worry about, most of which were far more serious than Sam's.

"I'm fine," she said.

Eileen's gaze slid with curiosity to the suitcase on the bed. "You're packing?"

"I'm leaving." In quick, brittle movements, Sam unzipped her suitcase, opened a dresser drawer and pulled out a handful of lingerie. She stuffed the bits and pieces into the suitcase.

"What about your date with Theo tonight?"

Sam shot Eileen an angry look. "Did you really tell Rogan that Theo and I would be a perfect match?"

Her brightly colored lips curled into a benign smile. "Clever of me, wasn't it?"

"Clever?" Sam sputtered. "What on earth makes

you think I'd want to go out with Theo—however nice he might be personally—much less consider marrying the man.''

''I don't.''

Her jaw going slack, Sam gaped at Eileen. ''But Rogan said—''

''Rogan is such a sweet man, and he's so confused. I do believe he's falling in love with you.''

Her jaw dropping even farther, Sam sat down heavily on the edge of the bed. ''That's ridiculous. Nothing I do pleases the man. I'm too athletic to be ladylike and too intelligent for his sensibilities.'' And he hadn't been all that impressed with her kisses, either, though Sam didn't feel a need to mention that.

''I suspect the attributes you just described are exactly the ones that appeal to Rogan. He's often dated vapid women, but they never last long. I believe you're quite a different sort and have managed to put him entirely off balance.''

Sam shook her head as if that would dislodge the fanciful notion Eileen was espousing. ''That doesn't make any sense. If he's in love with me, then he wouldn't be trying to pair me up with some other man, would he?''

''That's just the point. I posed the names of dozens of eligible bachelors to Rogan—men who I thought might be suitable for you. He found something wrong with every one of them. That's when I began to suspect he wasn't being honest with himself about his own feelings.''

Eileen sat next to Sam on the bed and took her hand. Softly she said, ''The question then becomes, how do you feel about Rogan?''

Lord help her, Sam didn't know. She was supposed to be gathering evidence to catch a thief. Instead she'd been getting emotionally involved with one of the suspects and embroiled in his family's affairs. Not exactly professional behavior. Clearly she was even more confused than Rogan.

"It seems to me, Eileen, that you ought to be warning me off of all the Prescott men, given your experience with your husband."

"Until recently I might have done just that. But these last few days staying here with you two..." She sighed and stared out the window at the sweep of the Santa Monica Bay. "I only wish Adam were as kind and considerate as Rogan."

"He likes to take in strays, I admit. We both appear to be included in that category. But that doesn't mean he'd be faithful if... well, if things got more serious."

"How can you say that? You've heard the phone ringing constantly. It's almost always a woman."

"Invariably." And each feminine voice on the answering machine had been like the prick of a dagger when Sam had heard it. "He's a playboy millionaire," she stated flatly. "Why wouldn't he have dozens of women falling at his feet?"

"How many of those women has he called back since you moved in with him?"

That stopped Sam. She couldn't recall him actually talking to any woman on the phone. Nor did she remember him paying any particular attention to the beautiful women at the parties they had attended together. Rogan had, in fact, always been very attentive to her. Under normal circumstances, the necklace he had just given her would mean—

But none of that really mattered. She and Rogan were light-years apart in social standing. He couldn't possibly have anything more than a platonic interest in the housekeeper's daughter—like the big brother he professed to be. To think otherwise was simply to delude herself.

Standing, Sam pulled open another dresser drawer and picked up a couple of sweaters.

"Go out with Theo," Eileen said firmly. "If I'm right, it might teach Rogan a very important lesson. This is how I think you ought to handle him."

In spite of herself, Sam listened. At the very least she might grab a few moments of sweet revenge. *If she could pull off Eileen's charade.*

ROGAN PACED the floor, aware of every sound that came from upstairs. He heard the shower turn on, pictured Sam stepping past the curtain into the tub, the warm water sluicing over her body, beading on her shoulders, clinging to the fine swell of her breasts.

His fingers clenched; he began to sweat. A dryness so thick he couldn't swallow filled his throat.

When the water stopped running, he imagined the fluffy white towel she was using, could see it skimming across her back and sliding the length of her shapely legs. He could smell the soft scent of her, taste her freshness.

His gaze shot to the phone.

He'd call Theo. *It's all a mistake, old friend. I've got other plans for Sam tonight. Better plans. Plans of my own.*

But Rogan couldn't do that. He needed to keep Sam safe. She wouldn't be safe with him. He'd love her…and then he'd destroy her life. That's what Prescotts did. How could he expect to break ranks with the grand family tradition of being a first-class scoundrel?

The floorboards squeaked above him and he knew she was dressing for her date with another man.

He shouldn't have listened to Eileen. Theo was all wrong for Sam. Too old. Too rich. Too attractive for a young woman to resist if she hadn't experienced much luxury in her life.

The doorbell rang, the sound jangling Rogan's raw nerves.

Damn! The guy was early. Why couldn't Theo have been stopped by a landslide that closed Pacific Coast Highway for a month?

Goofus lumbered down the stairs and, toenails clicking, marched across the wood floor to the door, his tail waving a friendly welcome.

A knot twisted in Rogan's gut. He could simply not answer the door and pretend no one was home. But he heard Sam moving upstairs, or maybe it was Eileen. One of them was bound to come down to see who was there.

A part of Rogan's brain shut down as he opened the door. It was the only way he could handle the thought of Sam going out with someone else. *The only way.*

HE WASN'T SURE how long he'd stood on the back deck before Eileen showed up. It had seemed like forever, waiting for Sam to come home. But maybe it had only been an hour. Maybe less.

"I called Martin," Eileen said. "He's coming by

to pick me up. I think it will be better if I stay with Aunt Agatha."

"You don't have to leave." Hell, for the last hour Rogan hadn't even been aware Eileen was in the house. Nothing had mattered except that Sam was with another man.

"Agatha has some ideas about where I can find a job. Her house is more centrally located for job hunting than Malibu is, and I do need to work."

"Yeah, well, maybe that's best." As much as he might like to distract himself with somebody else's problems tonight, he couldn't think about Eileen now. His brain was already on overload. "If you need anything, all you have to do is ask. You know that, don't you?"

"Yes, I do." She touched his arm lightly, but it wasn't the touch of the woman he wanted. "I think you need something, too, Rogan, and you won't let yourself even ask for it."

He looked around, at the dark ocean and his beachfront house with its oil paintings and resident dog for company. Suddenly none of it meant a damn thing to him. "Who could ask for more than all this?" he asked, mocking his life-style with a hint of bitterness.

"If you allow yourself, I think you'll come up with something." She smiled slyly. "My guess is that Sam will be home early. You might ask her if *she's* got any ideas."

Standing on tiptoe, Eileen kissed him goodbye. "You're a good man, Rogan. Give yourself a chance."

Rogan tried to think about that after Eileen left. But he kept seeing Sam with Theo, dancing with him, sipping champagne with him, and Rogan knew he was going to go crazy if she didn't come home soon.

At the first sound of a car stopping out front, Rogan raced for the door and yanked it open. He exhaled the breath he'd been holding the whole night.

Sam was standing on the porch, looking gorgeous and sexy, her red hair a tumble of curls, her body sleek and feminine. And she was alone.

"So what happened to Theo?" His voice felt thick and raw in his throat.

"I told him he didn't need to walk me to the door. He sort of twisted his ankle while we were dancing."

"Yeah? That's too bad." Denying himself the right to gloat, he backed up to let her in. "But you had a great time, right?" He was going to cut his own throat if she said yes.

She stepped a little closer and he swung the door closed behind her. "Before I left, Eileen suggested I tell you I'd had the best time of my life with Theo."

"Eileen's gone. Moved to Agatha's house."

"She must have planned all along to leave us alone."

"Possibly." He swallowed hard. Sam was wearing a tantalizing perfume he hadn't noticed before, some exotic scent that made him think of the South Seas and the fragrant breeze of an island paradise. "Did you?"

"I'd like for you to stop playing matchmaker, Rogan."

The blood drained from his face. "You've settled on Theo already?"

"No, I'm not going to marry Theo. Or anyone else right now."

"But you told me you were husband hunting."

"I lied." Smiling slightly, she leaned forward to brush a soft kiss to his lips. Eileen had given Sam the courage to reach for the golden ring, to test the limits of her feelings for Rogan. And his for her. Tonight with Theo she'd been reminded that not simply any man would do. She wanted the best—Rogan—for however long she might be able to hold him. "Is it so hard for you to imagine that you and I might want the same thing? And it isn't to get married."

Rogan's whole body tensed with the effort to control his instincts. "I can't give you forever, Sam. No Prescott male has been capable of that for three generations. Maybe more. And you're too fine a person to settle for less."

"Let me be the judge of that." She closed the slight distance between them, pressing her breasts against his chest. Only the thickness of her silky dress and his cotton shirt separated them.

Unbearable tautness gripped him, and his arms slid around her waist. She was sleek and supple beneath his hands. "Sam, you're killing me. I'm no good for you. Ever since we were kids—"

"I had a crush on you, you know."

"You did?" At his back he felt her tug his shirttail out of his pants, slip her hands underneath and knead her fingers along his spine. He groaned at the sheer pleasure of her touch.

"And I was desperately jealous when you brought a girlfriend home to meet your parents."

"That didn't happen often."

"Often enough to drive me crazy. I used to get so

mad at you when you teased me and treated me like a little kid. You were breaking my heart.''

"You were only eight years old.''

"I was thirteen the last time I saw you. You were a Harvard man, getting ready to graduate, and I was old enough to know how I felt.''

"I didn't mean to hurt you. It's just that you were so cute and blushed so easily.'' In spite of himself, Rogan nuzzled her sweet-smelling hair. The exotic scent aroused him, the silky texture like red flames licking away his good sense. Had there ever been another woman he'd wanted as much as Sam? He didn't think so. And yet he knew he was all wrong for her.

"And you thought of me as your little sister.''

"Yeah.'' He nibbled her earlobe and the word dragged out on a long sigh. She shuddered in response.

"I'm a grown woman now, Rogan.'' As if to emphasize the point, she shifted seductively against him, working her way into the nest of his hips, finding the hard ridge of his need. "And we're not even distantly related.''

"Not even kissin' cousins,'' he conceded.

"In that case, we could consider becoming lovers.''

"Sam—'' His voice broke. She didn't know what she was asking. "I want us to stay friends, and when lovers go their separate ways—''

"You're looking too far ahead, Rogan. Why can't we just enjoy the here and now?''

His heart missed a beat, then resumed with a heavy pulse. "I thought that was a man's line.'' He'd been guilty of using it more than once. He didn't want to do that to Sam, and felt a little strange that she had turned the tables on him.

"I believe in equal opportunity."

"You could be asking for an equal chance to make a mistake," he warned.

She brushed her lips across his in a series of fiery little kisses. "Nobody's asking for a guarantee. Life doesn't come that way."

"You're torturing me, Carrot Top." A sweet, sexy torture that was weakening his willpower. A man had to do what was right, but there were limits to what he could be asked to endure.

"We both know how we can end the misery, don't we?"

"Oh, yeah." Her eyes were the deepest green he had ever seen, her lips glossy and parted in sensual invitation.

"I trust Eileen got a ride to Agatha's house. She's gone now?"

He nodded absently and tried kissing Sam chastely, just a tease and a promise that he didn't intend to keep. But she'd have none of that.

Her tongue slid along the seam of his lips. Hunger knotted fiercely in his body. With a low rumble of desperate surrender deep in his throat, he opened his mouth and went recklessly on the attack. The kiss was deeper, more arousing, and more satisfying than any he had ever experienced.

Changing the angle and catching the back of her head in his hand, he probed moist, exciting recesses searching for her unique flavor.

She sighed a low, throaty purr as his hands kneaded her from scalp to nape, then lower still. She was no fragile flower but a wonderfully powerful woman who gave fully as much as she took, an equal partner in the mating dance.

Her eager response drove the last few bits of reason from his mind. His body throbbed with his need for her. He *had* to have Samantha Sterling—he needed her more than he needed air itself.

With shaking fingers, he tugged the straps of her dress from her shoulders. He palmed her full breasts in his hand.

She shuddered, sighing, "Yes. Oh, yes."

"Ah, Carrot Top, you're so beautiful. So perfect."

He lowered his head to kiss her there, on the blue-veined swell of flesh that had never seen the sun. He tasted her sweet, salty flavor.

"Theo asked me to go out with him again. Should I?"

"God, no, Sam. I couldn't stand it. Not again."

# *Chapter Eight*

His evening whiskers were rough beneath her eager fingertips, his scent musky and male, exciting her.

He plundered her mouth with his tongue. Sam matched him stroke for stroke. It was she who had learned the lesson tonight. Every man paled in comparison to Rogan. She recognized she'd always felt that way—all through her adolescence and in college, she'd compared each man she'd met to the one she had first loved. Rogan. None had measured up in her view.

And now, whatever the risk, she would take what she could. Enjoy what small piece of heaven he would grant her.

Her excitement rode on the crest of a wave that had been threatening for days, perhaps years. Now the seawall was ready to be breached. The tide lifted her toward the peak. Too soon, she realized, too impossibly soon.

Dimly she was aware of Rogan stripping her dress away, and her hungry need for his shirt to vanish in the same hurried fashion. In a heartbeat, her bra fell to the floor, no more than a soft whisper of cloth soon joined by his shirt.

"Oh, Rogan..." His name caught on a breath as he cupped her breast. Her fingers danced across his bare chest, teasing at the furring of hair she found there, the fine outline of muscle and sinew that she had admired from afar.

"My own Carrot Top." He suckled the nipple he'd bared, and his nickname for her took on a sultry sound that made Sam ache inside.

As though the weight of their combined desire could no longer hold them upright, they sank to the floor, to the roughly woven throw rug in front of the door. Goofus whined softly and padded off to some other place, giving them the privacy lovers deserved.

Rogan slid her panty hose down her legs, his hands touching her inner thighs, setting her on fire. "We could go upstairs."

"No. It would take too long." The need she felt was too irrepressible to have satisfaction delayed. Only Rogan could quell the urges he had created.

She writhed, helping him to remove the barrier of her clothes while she managed to work his cutoffs down over his lean hips. His arousal was magnificent. Briefly, she cupped him, but that wasn't enough. She wanted to feel him deep inside her, filling her, in a way she had only imagined until now.

Covering her with kisses, he groaned, "You are so beautiful."

In that moment, she believed him. She spread her legs to welcome him, aware only briefly of a slight delay while he pulled a packet from his hip pocket and took the precautions that she'd not even thought about.

Before she could register her gratitude, he dove into her slickness. She cried out and lifted her hips. His second thrust sent her over the edge. She flew to a place she had never been before. Her body pulsed, closing around him.

She opened her eyes as he sank into her one more time. Their eyes locked, and they raced together over the top with more force than an incoming tide. Waves of pleasure undulated through her and she felt his powerful response. Never before had it been like this.

Sobbing his name, she felt as though she had splintered into a thousand pieces. She sensed he followed her into that incredible sea of sensation as the essence of him pulsed through her.

Finally, after minutes had ticked by, her breathing eased, and her heartbeat resumed a normal rhythm. She stroked Rogan's back in lazy circles, his skin damp with perspiration. She licked his shoulder, tasting his salty flavor. His weight pressed her down. She cherished the feel of their bodies still linked together.

Slowly, as if he were returning from some other place, Rogan levered himself to his elbows and gazed down into Sam's eyes.

"I can't believe what we just did," he said, still breathless.

She threaded her fingers through his dark hair. "Don't you *dare* tell me what we just did was anything less than perfect."

The corners of his lips twitched and his gaze teased over her face. "You always do this sort of thing in the front entryway?"

"Sure. Don't you?" Making love with Rogan anywhere at all was fine with Sam.

He caught her and rolled them over so Sam was on top, straddling him. "Lady, *you* are a menace. You could drive a guy crazy."

"Good."

"More than good," he agreed. "Now the problem is, how do I get you upstairs without letting go of you. See, I was listening to you take a shower earlier...and, well, this time we're going to do it together."

Impossibly, Sam felt a new flutter of excitement when she'd thought sure she'd been entirely sated by their frantic coming together. But her desire flared almost as quickly as it had the first time. "You're a very creative man. I'm sure you'll think of something."

He stirred inside her. "You're a hard woman to please, Carrot Top, but I'll do my best."

It wasn't as easy as Rogan had hoped, but with several long pauses on the stairs to kiss and touch, they finally made their way to the bathroom off the master bedroom. He turned on the shower and adjusted the water.

Sam's lids were heavy, the sexy eyes of a passionate woman. He wanted to taste her and fondle her everywhere at once, give her all the passion she could handle. But he was already near the brink again.

"I want to go slow this time," he said as they stepped into the oversize tile stall and he pulled the door shut behind them. The clear glass immediately began to fog with steam as three shower heads delivered a gentle pelting of warm water over them. "But I'm not sure I can."

"You don't have to go slow on my account." She palmed his already full arousal. "I promise I'll keep up."

Rogan stifled a groan at her touch. Her eager response heightened his own, and he felt a new urgency build within him. Taking a bar of soap, he lathered his hands, then laved the bubbles over her shoulders and breasts, down her flat stomach. His fingers searched through the thatch of copper hair at the apex of her thighs to discover the sensitive nub that was hidden there.

She gasped as he circled her, the experience of giving her pleasure profoundly satisfying for him.

"Oh, my…Rogan!" Trembling, she clasped her arms around his neck, her body slick with soap against his, breasts pressed to his chest as they stood thigh to thigh.

"You feel so good."

"I want you…inside me."

"Yes." He wanted that, too, as he had never wanted it before. That it was Sam who made him burn with such intensity was a fact he couldn't change. Nor could he alter the truth that he was wrong for her. But he couldn't deal with that now, or worry about tomorrow, not when her hands were skimming over him like flames that refused to be quenched by the falling water.

Placing his hands at her waist, he lifted her, braced her against the shower wall and thrust into her. She sobbed his name, her body convulsed around him, and his own control shattered as though this were their first time all over again.

BONELESS.

That's how Sam felt as she woke to find herself curled next to Rogan in his king-size bed, the morning overcast muting the sunlight that flowed in through the open window, the sound of the ocean distant and soothing. His chest rose and fell in a steady rhythm beneath her hand. Their scents had mingled as their bodies had melded during the night, mixing their musk in an erotic aroma that still hovered in the room.

How many times had they made love? she wondered. Given the tenderness between her legs, she didn't even want to venture a guess.

Remembering her total lack of inhibition, she smiled and a flush rose to her cheeks. Last night had been a rare experience. Her only regret was that it couldn't be a forever thing with Rogan. Knowing the Prescott family, Sam knew he was being honest with her that faithfulness didn't run in his genes.

But after living with him for these past two weeks and seeing firsthand his generosity—and after their lovemaking last night—it hurt doubly to admit there'd be no forevers. Still, she had known of his failing when she'd suggested they become lovers. Now she'd have to live with it.

He moved, groaning softly, and his arm tightened around her shoulders.

Rogan had been honest with her since the beginning, she mused. There'd been no effort at deceit; he had no wish for marriage or commitment.

In return, she had lied to him about who she was

and what she did for a living. How would he respond, she wondered, when he learned she was a cop—one who had been trying to prove *he* was a thief?

A band of fear wrapped itself around her and threatened to squeeze the air from her lungs. What if he hated her when he learned of her deception?

The brush of his lips across her forehead brought tears to her eyes. God, she hated secrets. Hers most of all.

"You ready to face a new day?" he asked, his voice husky with sleep.

"Only because there's no other choice."

"Hmm. We could just drop out for a week or so. The answering machine is on. I can disconnect the doorbell." He nuzzled the side of her neck, his whiskers rough like his voice.

"Sounds tempting." But Sam had to talk to Garcia. While the investigation was still pending, she needed her supervisor's permission to reveal her identity to Rogan. She couldn't go on with this lie any longer, whatever his reaction might be. It simply wasn't fair.

Goofus decided to veto the idea of their lingering in bed any longer.

In response to their voices, he padded into the room and jumped onto the bed. Sam grunted as the dog walked across her middle and stood staring down at Rogan. He licked his face.

"Aw, mutt, get outta here." Rogan pulled the sheet up over his head.

She giggled. "Looks like Goofus thinks we ought to get going. He's probably hungry."

"He's always hungry."

Grumbling, Rogan gave her a quick kiss then rolled

out of bed, totally unconcerned by his nakedness. He had a beautiful body, lean and hard, and tight buns that would earn him a "ten" from any woman.

"You want breakfast in bed?" he asked as he pulled on some trousers, neglecting to snap the top fastening.

Unintentionally, her gaze zeroed in on that slight omission. "No, I'll come downstairs. Give me a minute to get dressed."

He eyed her speculatively. "Too bad, I was hoping you'd agree to holing up in bed with me for about a year. I was just getting started last night."

Laughing, she said, "Nobody has that much endurance, Prescott. Not even you."

"It'd be a hell of a lot of fun to try, though." With a cocky grin, he leaned over and kissed her again. "You know what we *are* going to do today?"

"Give me a clue."

"We're going to cash in on the weekend yachting trip I won at Agatha's fancy party."

Her eyes widened. "We are? How? The weekend's half-over. Besides, wouldn't we have to make arrangements ahead of time?"

"Not a chance. The yacht's mine and what I say goes."

"You mean you bid some exorbitant price to win a weekend on your own boat?"

"Hey, what ship's captain would want strangers messing around on his boat? I figured the best thing I could do was outbid all the competition."

Laughing, Sam linked her arms around his neck and pulled him back down onto the bed. He was impossible, incredible, the most wonderful man she'd ever known. Confessions and Garcia could wait. For the rest of the weekend she'd simply put her career on hold, along with her heart.

What could two days hurt?

THEY MADE IT back from Catalina by mid-morning on Monday. Sam stretched languorously as she went up to her room to shower and change. An abbreviated weekend wasn't nearly long enough, she decided. To count on being with Rogan more than one day at a time, however, seemed impossible. And that's what she wanted most.

She battled the ache in her chest that had threatened to spread all weekend. She had gone into this with her eyes wide open. For the first time in her life, she'd even been the aggressor. Now she'd have to reap what she had sown, good or bad.

In her room, she dressed in slacks, a comfortable blouse and her sturdy work shoes. She'd go in to the office this morning and get Garcia to reassign her to some other case, or send her back to patrol duty. Then she'd be able to tell Rogan the truth. Her own ethics demanded honesty. She'd already delayed too long.

As she started downstairs, she heard a phone ring. The sound was oddly muffled, not like it was Rogan's phone at all. More like—

In a few quick strides, she was across the room and pulled open a dresser drawer. She reached into her purse to retrieve her cell phone, flipped it open and said, "Yes?"

"Where the hell have you been the past two days?" Garcia's voice bellowed in her ear.

She winced, realizing she hadn't given the investigation a whole lot of thought for the past forty-eight hours. Maybe she wasn't cut out for police work after all. "With Rogan," she hedged. "Where else?"

"I've been calling your phone and leaving messages on his, for all the good it did. If you hadn't picked up this time, I was going to send a black-and-white to check on you. What the hell have you been doing?"

"Oh, this and that." *A little sailing and a whole lot of making love.* "What did you want?"

"We got our thief."

"You what?"

"There was another necklace snatched Friday night—an incident you missed entirely," he stressed. "The guy showed up Saturday in Santa Monica to sell it. This time we got there in time and nailed him dead-to-rights."

"Who is it?"

"You can find out when you get here. I want you to bring Rogan in with you."

"Is he implicated in the thefts?"

"Listen up, Sterling. Just get your butt down here. We need to get to the bottom of this."

The connection went dead, leaving Sam staring at the instrument like it was a foreign object. Was Garcia planning to arrest Rogan? Dear God, she hoped not.

And had she just blown her entire career?

MYRIAD THOUGHTS overwhelmed Sam as they drove to the West L.A. station—about her career, about Rogan, and her future. Her mind swirled with confusion.

Recognizing the officer at the front desk, without

thinking Sam flashed her ID in his direction as she had so many times when she arrived at the office. He waved Rogan and her on through, and she headed for the stairs.

Rogan snared her by the arm before she could open the door to the stairwell. He was still wearing his sailing clothes, his cotton shirt open at the collar, his pleated trousers baggy and comfortable-looking. His leather sandals slapped against the hardwood floor when he walked.

"What do you think you're doing, Sam?" he whispered under his breath. "It's one thing for me to con a jewelry store owner in Bakersfield with a phony ID, but you can't go trotting into a police station on your own. You've got to sign in and be escorted, or something. That's what we did last time."

Sam's shoulders slumped. She'd been so caught up in discovering who the thief was, she'd lost her concentration. But it was too late now. And it was well past time for the truth to come out.

"Rogan, I'm a police officer, a member of the L.A.P.D. My ID is real. I'm authorized to escort you upstairs."

His blue eyes narrowed and his shoulders went rigid. "What the hell are you talking about?"

Taking him by the arm, she said, "I'll explain everything later. First, let's talk to Garcia and find out what's going on."

Rogan came to his senses by the time they reached the first landing. He halted abruptly. "Wait a minute. You're telling me you're a cop?"

She was standing on the stair above him so he had

to look up into her clear green eyes. "Yes. I've been working undercover these past few weeks."

"Investigating me?"

"Among other suspects. Yes," she said softly, apologetically. "I've been working on the rash of jewelry thefts."

Their voices echoed strangely in the stairwell, the sound bouncing off the concrete walls and steps. Rogan's mind worked sluggishly trying to make sense of what Sam was saying along with all the images that came to mind.

"That's why you carry a gun?"

"It's one of several I own. On duty, I have to carry one. That's standard operating procedure."

He nodded, something painful twisting through his gut. Things were beginning to fall into place but he didn't much like the picture that was forming. "And the guy you took down at Bakersfield gas station? You did that so easily because you're a cop."

"I told you I had training."

"Yeah. You did. I figured you meant judo classes." He speared his fingers through his hair. "You knew that and you let me believe it anyway."

"I couldn't explain. Not then."

"So you lied." He'd thought Sam was different—different from the plastic, superficial people who had filled his life until now, those who brushed elbows with the Prescotts and always tried to take something away. God, he thought he'd known Sam. Now, he realized, it had all been an illusion.

"It was my job, Rogan. I'm sorry."

"I bet." He glanced at the door to the second floor, a huge sense of betrayal corkscrewing his gut into a knot. He'd slept with Sam, for God's sake, and all the time she'd been *investigating* him like a common criminal. In a dozen ways, she'd lied to him. Maybe even her sleeping with him had been part of the same charade—giving new meaning to *undercover*, he thought grimly. "Is Garcia planning to arrest me?"

"I don't know. He just said he wanted me to bring you in."

Maybe Garcia wanted that but Rogan wanted to break Sam's neck—or toss her over his shoulder and take her back to his house and lock them inside, forgetting what he had just learned. But he couldn't do that.

"I suppose I owe you thanks for not bringing me into the station in handcuffs."

"I don't think it's like that, Rogan."

"No? Why not? Didn't you come up with enough evidence against me to issue a warrant?"

"I eliminated you as a suspect a long time ago. You don't have a motive, and for the heist that happened over the weekend, I'm your alibi."

"Convenient, isn't it? Or maybe I'm smart and I have an accomplice who does all the dirty work."

She raised her eyebrows. "Do you?"

She was a real piece of work. He'd never guessed, never once suspected, she was anything but what she'd pretended to be. *Or what you wanted her to be,* a small voice inside him suggested.

He swore and brushed past her to the door. "Come on, let's get this over with. I want to get out of here."

Sam started to call his name, but it died in her throat. She hadn't wanted to tell him the truth this way; she'd wanted to ease into it by talking about how she'd felt it necessary to go along with whatever Garcia had ordered. For her career. For her friends who had died. But she'd missed her chance. The damage was done. She'd seen the anger in Rogan's eyes, the betrayal he'd felt.

She didn't blame him. But it did hurt that their fragile relationship, as new as this morning's sunrise, might well have been shattered beyond repair.

ROGAN GAZED through the two-way mirror into the interrogation room.

"You've arrested Martin? Aunt Agatha's chauffeur? My God, you must be out of your mind." Martin, usually so impeccably dressed, looked frazzled, his tie loose at his collar, his hair unkempt, his dark suit jacket tossed over the back of the chair. His fingers trembled as he reached for a disposable foam cup on the table.

"We don't have the wrong man, Mr. Prescott." Garcia leaned laconically against the wall of the observation room, his arms crossed. He had a beady look in his eyes, like a predator about to leap on his prey. "We've got him dead-to-rights on possession of stolen goods. The only question is how he got them."

"Martin has never stolen anything in his life. He's been with Aunt Agatha for more than twenty-five years. She trusts him implicitly. The man is no more a thief than I am."

"The thought has occurred to us that he might not be the mastermind of the thievery ring. It could be somebody else, somebody who had better access to the women who've been losing their jewelry. Somebody who is part of the same social set."

Rogan glared at the detective, then snapped a glance to where Sam was standing at the back of the small room, so close he could catch a trace of her fragrant South Seas scent. Her betrayal still hurt. It probably would for a long time. It would help if she didn't look so incredibly professional—so coplike— in a tailored jacket that cleverly disguised her shoulder holster. He'd been such a damn fool! What other woman had he ever known who carried a piece?

What other woman had he ever wanted with such total reckless abandon?

"If you're planning to arrest me, Garcia, then do it. Otherwise, I'm out of here. And within thirty minutes, Martin will be free, too. I plan to call my lawyer."

"Officer Sterling tells me—rightly or wrongly— that you're not a viable suspect. What I'd rather have from you is to go in there with Martin and talk to him. He's not a youngster, Lord knows. I don't think he wants to take this fall alone. With as many counts of grand theft as we have against him, he'll be a hundred and two before he gets out of the slammer." Garcia shoved himself away from the wall. "What we want to know is who is behind all these thefts. We want the big enchilada. The mastermind. With his testimony, we can cut Martin a deal."

"It's the best thing you can do, Rogan," Sam encouraged. "The description the Bakersfield jewelry store owner gave us fits Martin to a tee, including the British accent."

Rogan didn't want to listen to her. But Martin, normally a man of great dignity, looked so pathetic sitting there at that scarred table. Why the hell would he have gone to Bakersfield to sell an emerald necklace?

His teeth clenched. "All right, I'll talk to him. But I won't guarantee any results."

Garcia flashed him a smile that lacked even a small touch of friendliness. "Officer Sterling will join you during the interrogation."

"I'd rather she didn't."

The detective's lips curled derisively. "Indulge me. She needs the experience."

Sam fumed as she followed Rogan into the interrogation room a few minutes later. It was rare to have a civilian interview a suspect, equally unusual that a patrol officer would be involved. But in this case, it made sense. Nonetheless, she hated that Garcia had put her in this awkward position. She hated that her job had made it necessary. But most of all, she hated that she'd lied to Rogan.

Martin stood immediately. "Oh, sir, I'm so very glad you've come." His rather frantic gaze flicked over to Sam. "And you, Miss Sterling. What a dreadful situation. Truly dreadful."

"Sit down, Martin." Rogan cupped the chauffeur's shoulder in a reassuring gesture. "I'm sure this is some stupid bureaucratic mistake and we'll be able to straighten everything out in no time. Not for a minute do I believe you've stolen any jewels."

"No, sir, indeed not. I would never do such a terrible thing. Never." Clearly on the verge of hysteria, Martin shook his head vigorously. "I'm so glad you believe me."

"Of course, Martin," Rogan said soothingly as he sat down next to the man. "Just calm down and tell me why on earth the cops think you were trying to hock stolen jewels."

"Because they caught me. Oh, mercy, whatever will happen to me?"

Rogan frowned. "Did you know they'd been stolen?"

"Certainly not." He looked affronted at the mere possibility. "I would never knowingly be a party to such a thing. Never."

Sam crossed the room and took a chair across the table from Martin. She covered his hand with hers. "If that's true, Martin, then you must tell us who gave you the jewels."

He straightened his spine with quiet dignity and lifted his chin, sitting so erect a normal person's spine would break. His eyelids fluttered. "I'm afraid I can't do that, miss. I *am* sorry."

"You've got to tell us, Martin," Rogan said. "They're gonna nail you with the whole damn series of jewel thefts if you don't come clean."

Paling visibly, the chauffeur shook his head. "I do apologize, sir, but it's simply not possible. I fear I must *clam up*, as they say on the telly."

Sam rolled her eyes. She'd seen enough interrogations to know this man wasn't going to talk. He might as well have had a steel rod in his spine. He wasn't going to bend. Lighted toothpicks under his fingernails wouldn't persuade him. Martin wasn't about to give them any information because, she suspected, the person behind the thefts was someone to whom he owed his absolute allegiance.

In her view, that could only be one person. She dreaded the possibility.

Rogan continued to try to cajole information out of Martin. It wasn't doing any good.

"Come on," she told him finally. "Let's leave Martin to his thoughts for a while. Maybe he'll reconsider." Though she doubted that was possible, however long he was made to wait in this dreary place.

She all but had to force Rogan out of the room and into the hallway. She glanced up and down the stark corridor, relieved they were alone.

"Someone is using Martin," Rogan assured her. "That man doesn't have a criminal bone in his body."

"You're probably right. That's why I think we should go have a talk with your aunt Agatha."

He gaped at her as if she'd lost her mind. "Involving Martin in all of this isn't enough for you people? Now you want to drag Aunt Agatha into this mess, too?"

She cringed at his including her in the derogatory phrase "you people," though it was probably well deserved. "Think about it, Rogan. You and I can go have a heart-to-heart with Agatha. If she doesn't know anything about the jewels that were stolen, then no one is the wiser. But if she is involved, you'll be able to take remedial action before Garcia is even aware of the possibility." She checked the hallway again. "And if you tell anyone I suggested that, I'll deny it. Trying to circumvent the system would cost me my job."

He glared at her, his eyes dark with the promise of throttling her with his bare hands at the very first opportunity. But she could also see his mind working, shifting through what they knew, and finally coming to the same conclusion she had.

"Damn!" he muttered and turned away.

She followed him down the hallway past a portrait gallery of former station commanders. Few of the photos were flattering. Not one was female.

# Chapter Nine

Sam waited impatiently as Rogan pressed the doorbell a second time. He'd been silent and grim during the entire drive to Agatha's house. Not that Sam could blame him. The shocking fact that his aunt, charming, dotty Agatha, might be a thief had stunned Sam, too. Added to the news that Sam was a cop, Rogan's mood was understandable.

But she did wish his anger hadn't been quite so palpable. They needed to talk—if not now, certainly later.

Aunt Agatha peered out through the peephole, then pulled the door open wide, beaming them a welcome. "Dear boy! What a surprise. And Sam. How nice," she crooned. She'd evidently been gardening because she had on a broad-brimmed straw hat and carried a pair of work gloves and clippers in her hand.

"We were beginning to think you weren't home," Rogan said, bending to kiss his aunt's cheek.

"Oh, mercy, Juanita was busy in the kitchen, and I'm so used to Martin answering the door, when he's not here I'm a bit slow."

"That's why we've come. To talk about Martin."

"You know, it's quite troubling." She stopped in the entryway, distractedly straightening a small sculpture that sat on an antique table with an exquisite inlaid wood design. "He told me he was planning to visit friends over the weekend, but I did think he'd be back by this morning." She looked up hopefully. "Do you suppose he was visiting a *lady* friend and was delayed?"

"I don't think so, Aunt Agatha." He cupped her elbow, ushering her into a family parlor off the hallway. She looked a bit bemused as he seated her in a comfortable chair. Sam sat nearby while Rogan continued to pace.

"Where's Eileen?" Rogan asked, apparently not ready to deal with the reason for their visit just yet.

"Oh, she's off at an interview. Bruce Hinkley, that dear man who runs that big movie studio over in Burbank, needs a receptionist. I thought Eileen would be perfect for the job. Don't you? She's so eager to get her life on track again. Poor dear. And that naughty boy, Adam. We'll just have to see that he takes his responsibilities seriously from now on. Prescott men, even my dear Arnold, God rest his soul, can be so thoughtless." She shook her head and tsked. "Shameful, that's what it is."

"I'm glad Eileen has you to help her out," Rogan said.

Sam interrupted, preferring to stick with the subject that had brought them here—and not wanting to be reminded of the imperfect virtues of Prescott males. "Agatha, we've come to tell you that Martin has been arrested."

Her pale blue eyes widened. In an anxious gesture,

her hand flew to her hair, smoothing the flyaway strands of gray back under her hat. "Whatever for?" she asked.

"Sam and I thought maybe you could help us out on that."

Agatha blinked rapidly. "I have no idea. Why, he's as stalwart and reliable as they come. Surely there's been some mistake."

"Possibly." Sam leaned back in her chair and tented her fingers in front of her lips. Agatha was lying. That much was obvious from her nervous gestures. But how deep her involvement was in the thefts was difficult to ascertain. "Did you stay overnight when you went to Bakersfield with Martin, or did you come back the same day?"

Agatha stared at her blankly, the question obviously catching her off guard. "I don't believe I've ever been to Bakersfield, my dear. Oh, I've driven past it a time or two on the highway, I suppose, but I've never actually been into the city."

"But you must have." Based on what the jewelry store owner had said, Sam was sure the passenger in Martin's limousine had been Agatha, and she'd fully expected the older woman to fall into her verbal trap.

But if it wasn't Agatha in the car, who else could it have been?

"Juanita visits her relatives in Bakersfield once or twice a year," Agatha continued, "but I've had no reason to go along."

Sam's head snapped up and her gaze collided with Rogan's. *Juanita?* she mouthed.

He shrugged, as if to say, "Anything is possible."

Agitated, Agatha alternately fussed with, then

smoothed the fingers of her work gloves. "Rogan, dear, you really must see about Martin. He's not a criminal, you know. Truly he's not."

"I know, Agatha, and I'm trying to take care of it."

Standing, Sam said, "You say Juanita is in the kitchen?"

"Yes. At least she was a few minutes ago."

Sam gestured with her head in that direction, inviting Rogan to join her in the kitchen. "Let's go have a talk with her."

They left Agatha in the parlor looking thoroughly puzzled and more confused than usual, if that were possible.

"This whole thing is crazy," Rogan said. His leather sandals slapped on the hardwood floor of the hallway. "None of these people is a criminal. I've known them all my life. I'd stake my entire wealth on their innocence."

"Don't risk it. It's possible you don't know them at all."

He slanted her a glance. "I sure as hell didn't have *your* number right, did I?"

The bitterness in his tone sent Sam's heart slamming against her ribs, and her stomach knotted. "I'm sorry I had to lie to you. If you hadn't caught me breaking into Geoffrey's safe—"

"Was he a suspect, too?"

"Yes. Particularly after we learned the man who was pawning the jewelry had a British accent."

"It figures," he mumbled.

"We had ten or fifteen possible suspects." She

frowned. "Strangely, neither Martin nor Juanita was on the list."

"Why the hell not? Everybody else I know apparently made your top ten."

Her steps slowed. "Because Martin and Juanita were not on the guest lists of the parties where the jewels were stolen. And they weren't working for the caterers, either."

"There. You see? They probably have an alibi."

"But Martin was caught red-handed with a diamond necklace that didn't belong to him," she argued as much for her own benefit as Rogan's. "If he didn't actually take the jewels, then someone else did and was using him to sell them. It doesn't exactly seem logical that Juanita would be the mastermind behind all this."

"You've got that right."

They found Juanita in the kitchen creating a fluffy confection she told them she planned to serve to Agatha's cohorts in the philanthropy world at a meeting scheduled for later that afternoon.

Unable to resist, Rogan stuck his finger into the sweet, sugary mix, then licked it off. "Delicious," he proclaimed.

"It is not for you, young man." Trying—and failing—to look stern, the cook halfheartedly swatted at his hand. She smiled pleasantly at Sam. "He was always this way as a boy, his fingers into every pie. He needs a good woman to keep him out of mischief."

A flush rose to Sam's cheeks and she let her gaze slide past Juanita to the view of a sparkling pool outside and the immaculately landscaped garden. Her chances of being that woman were somewhere between zero and none. The housekeeper's daughter and the millionaire playboy? Not likely at all.

Clearing the lump that formed in her throat, she said, "Juanita, we need to ask you some questions."

"Yes. Of course." She ladled a spoonful of the creamy mixture into a pastry shell. Her bib apron was spotless, while Sam would have been a mess from head to toe if she'd been working with such a gooey concoction.

"When you visit your relatives in Bakersfield, does Martin drive you there?" she asked.

"Sometimes, yes. If he does not have to drive the missus somewhere."

"Did he take you there about a month ago?"

She shrugged, still concentrating on filling the pastry shells. "I do not know. I sometimes lose track of the weeks."

Rogan said, "Juanita, this is important. Did you stop at a jewelry store in Bakersfield when you were with Martin the last time?"

She looked up at Rogan, her forehead furrowed, her dark eyes clear of any deceit. "He said he had an errand to run for the missus. Was there something wrong there?"

Sam patted the older woman on the arm. "No, everything is fine, Juanita. Thank you for telling us."

Sam turned away, planning to retrace her steps and find Agatha in the main part of the house.

"Wait, Sam," Rogan ordered, following her from the kitchen.

"It's your aunt," Sam said firmly. "I'm sorry, Rogan, but it has to be her. She was on every single one of those guest lists but no one thought—"

Within a few short strides, Rogan snared Sam by the arm and hauled her up short, dragging her hard against his body. He hadn't bothered to shave that morning before they'd sailed back from Catalina and there was a light stubble of whiskers on his cheeks. "I want you to leave my family alone."

She gasped, the icy anger in his eyes and the taut set of his jaw taking her breath away. While she could admire his loyalty to his family, she couldn't go along with what he wanted. "I can't. I'm a sworn officer of the law."

He glared at her, his chest moving with each breath he took, his control on the edge of breaking. She caught the exact moment he realized how close they were standing to each other, their bodies touching from shoulder to hip. The word *lover* vibrated in the air between them, taunting Sam with images of Rogan's body over hers. Under hers.

*A part of her.*

Deep down, her body clenched in response to her memories.

The hallway was narrow; there seemed no way to escape the emotions that had buffeted her since he'd learned of her lie.

Sam couldn't believe how much it hurt that her small piece of forever with Rogan had been cut so short—less than a full weekend.

"How long?" he asked roughly.

She blinked. *Not nearly long enough.*

"How long have you been a cop?" he repeated.

"Oh." She'd been considering another question entirely. "It's been about six weeks since I graduated from the academy. They pulled me off of patrol duty for this undercover assignment."

"Congratulations." He said it grimly, as though she'd been assigned to sorting through a garbage dump.

"This assignment was a real coup. Rookies don't usually get to work undercover." Not that she'd done much real investigative work, stuck as she'd been at Rogan's house—falling in love with her host and prime suspect.

"Wonderful." Releasing Sam, Rogan stepped away. He couldn't touch her without remembering the silken feel of her bare skin against his, couldn't look into her eyes without recalling how deep a green they became, almost black, when she was aroused.

He remembered tunneling his fingers through the tangle of her tousled copper curls and, in spite of everything, he wanted to do it again, kiss her until they were both beyond reason.

Damn, what a mess he was in!

And so was Aunt Agatha.

"What good will it do anyone if you put my aunt behind bars?"

"None, probably. But that's not my decision to make."

"Yeah, right."

She lifted her stubborn little chin defiantly. Her eyes sparked with green fireworks. "I'm part of that thin blue line that protects people and their property in this town, Rogan. And I'm darn proud of it. If people I like break the law, that's too bad. It's my job to arrest them just like I would anybody else."

"Even your own grandmother, I suppose."

"Even her." She returned his gaze levelly.

She wouldn't back down. Rogan knew that. Under other circumstances, he might have admired her attitude. But this was his aunt she was talking about.

He pushed past her. God, he didn't want to see Agatha in jail. And that's where all of this was heading, as much as he'd like to believe otherwise.

He found Agatha arranging flowers in the dining room, snapdragons and gladioli, carnations and Boston ferns that she'd cut herself, all from her own garden. Her hat was tilted at an unsettling angle; her hands shook as she fussed with the flowers.

His throat tightened as he remembered the hours he'd spent as a kid helping her tend her garden. He didn't suppose he'd been all that useful, but she'd made him feel like he had some small purpose in life—to make the flowers grow, to create something beautiful. Now he felt as though he was going to crush the loveliest bloom of all, his wonderful, generous aunt.

With effort, he cleared the lump from his throat. "Aunt Agatha, I need for you to be straight with me." Gently, he took a bright red gladiolus from her hand and laid it on the table. "Are you the one who's been stealing jewelry from all those people?"

She picked up the flower and stuffed it into the center of the arrangement. "If those dreadful people hadn't been so parsimonious, I wouldn't have needed to *take* the jewelry. They would have given me what I needed."

*Parsimonious?* "What are you talking about, Aunt Agatha?"

"Like Monica Lankershim. She spends gobs of

money on plastic surgery for herself—which does no good at all—and then she won't contribute so much as a single penny to a worthy cause. So selfish of her.''

"I'm not following you, Agatha." Though he did remember Monica Lankershim had lost a diamond necklace at the party where he'd met Sam.

"Chandler House, dear boy. What else?''

"You've contributed thousands upon thousands of dollars to that outfit. Why would you have to steal to give more?''

"Because…oh, my." Her hands fluttered around the flowers, straightening here, bending there, shaping the bouquet into an artistic arrangement. "I'm not a criminal, you know. Not really. I simply didn't have any more to give, don't you see? I haven't been very frugal with the money Arnold left me. Not really. But there are so many others who are needy, and I desperately didn't want Chandler House to suffer because of my failing. The program is so important. All those young people at risk. And if I couldn't provide them with any more money…" Tears sprang to her eyes. "They might not want me to serve on their board of directors any longer, don't you see?''

Rogan did see. Without funds to contribute to her causes, Agatha felt no one would want her. She'd operated on the basis of cash in exchange for love for so many years, she no longer realized her own personal value to any organization. In a tragic way, she had prostituted herself for the people and causes she cared about.

Moment by moment, Agatha appeared to become more agitated. Rogan wasn't sure of his aunt's health and he grew concerned at the high color on her cheeks and her rapid breathing. He pulled out a chair and helped her to sit down.

Kneeling beside her, Sam took Agatha's hand, surreptitiously taking her pulse. "There's something I don't understand."

"What's that, dear girl?"

"At the fund-raising party I attended with Rogan, a pair of diamond earrings found their way into my purse. Do you know how they got there?"

"Oh, my…" Her hand flying to her throat, Agatha laughed as though she'd just played an extraordinary joke on someone—perhaps herself. "I wondered what had happened. You see, I thought I'd put those in *my* purse. But I was so busy with all our VIP guests and getting everyone settled in their places, I must have mistaken your purse for mine. Our tables were right next to each other, you'll remember. And then they announced the earrings were missing. Well, don't you just know I thought I'd been caught. Frightening, really. Then I checked my purse and they weren't there. Land sakes, I was relieved. But I couldn't imagine—"

"Rogan found them. That's how they ended up under the silent-auction table."

"What a dear boy." She reached over to squeeze Rogan's hand.

Sam met Rogan's gaze. At least one mystery was solved, that small bit of misunderstanding that had led Sam to move in with him—to allow herself to be "rescued" by him. At the moment, only her heart needed rescuing. She doubted Rogan would volunteer for the job this time.

"Agatha."

The older woman lifted her head in response to her name.

"Did you, by chance, keep track of all the people you stole from and what you took?" he asked.

"Of course, dear boy. When you're in the business of charities, it's ever so important to keep good records. And I always listed those who had contributed their jewelry as donors to the cause. Some of them have their names on quite nice plaques on the wall. That was the fair thing to do, don't you think?"

"Including those whose jewels you took in Florida?" Sam asked on a hunch.

Agatha's eyes widened. "My, my, you know about those people, too?"

"Yes, ma'am. We do." It made Sam a little sick to her stomach to realize how much Agatha had stolen over the past several years, despite the fact that it might have been for a good cause.

"Aunt Agatha, when Martin took the jewels to sell them, did he know they were stolen?"

"Goodness, no. I wouldn't involve him in such a thing. Years ago he pawned my own jewels for me— until I ran out and had nothing left but paste. Then when I needed more money..." She shrugged, looking sheepish. "I made sure he thought all the jewels were mine and I was simply cashing in the old bits and pieces I had around the house, family heirlooms. He never questioned me. He's quite loyal, you see."

Rogan understood, in some obscure way. What he needed now, however, was a plan that would keep Aunt Agatha from spending the rest of her life behind bars. He had the troubling feeling, one way or another, it was going to cost him a great deal of money. Not that it wouldn't be money well spent.

Deep in thought, he flinched when Sam touched his arm.

"I think you ought to call your attorney," she said softly. "He can arrange for Agatha to surrender to the police. Things will go more smoothly if she does."

Her suggestion, however reasonable, tore at his gut and he responded gruffly. "What? You don't want to handcuff her and haul her in yourself? Maybe you could get a headline in the tabloids—Undercover Cop Nails Thief. That ought to earn you lots of points with Garcia."

Sam hated the bitterness in his voice, but she understood. She only wished it didn't hurt so much.

IT FIGURED Agatha would know the district attorney personally.

The D.A., Rogan, Agatha and her attorney had been in an upstairs conference at the police station for hours. At loose ends, Sam paced, drank black coffee and got more anxious by the minute. By now they could have plea-bargained a serial killer, for heaven's sake! What the devil was taking them so long?

"Hey, Sam." Bobby Jackson sauntered into the squad room. His slick jacket looked like he'd slept in it. "I hear you made a collar on the Westside jewel thief."

"That's right. The D.A. is talking to her now."

Loosening his tie, he sat in the chair behind his cluttered desk, tipped back and propped his feet on an open drawer. One of his shoes showed signs of a hole developing in the sole. "You don't look too happy about it."

She shrugged. "It's someone I care about." She cared about Aunt Agatha's nephew even more, for all the good it would do her.

"Not that Rogan Prescott character, I hope."

By force of will she didn't let her expression change. For a woman on the force, a hard exterior was crucial to survival. She didn't dare give away her emotions. "His aunt."

"No fooling?" He laughed. "That dotty old lady's been running circles around the force for months?"

Two other detectives came into the room. One tossed his jacket over the clothes rack.

"Hey, guys," Jackson said. "Our rookie here nailed the perp in the jewelry case. Would you believe it was an eighty-year-old woman with more than one screw loose who had us chasing our tails?"

Sam bristled. "She's a sweet woman. Just a bit misguided, is all. Her intentions were honorable enough." Hardly the kind of hardened criminal Sam had envisioned arresting when she joined the force.

"They all claim that," the second detective said. "Particularly the ones who are one sandwich short of a full picnic. The victims don't usually see it the same way."

"She didn't actually hurt anyone," Sam proclaimed. But no one was listening.

Picking up a stack of phone messages, Jackson sorted through them. "Linkowski, some broad left word you're to call her. She sounded like a *reeaal* sweetheart."

"Hey, give me that!" Linkowski dived for the message slip.

The two men wrestled for a moment, making lewd comments about the woman in question. They'd forgotten Sam was anywhere around and weren't the least impressed she'd solved a crime.

At the moment, neither was Sam. She'd caught a criminal who had the world's biggest heart, had betrayed the man she loved, and her fellow police officers had already dismissed her as a rookie who didn't belong in the lofty world of real detectives.

The thought that Jackson and his cohorts were right nearly brought Sam to her knees.

Maybe she wasn't cut out to be a cop. *Too soft*, a nagging voice taunted.

But she'd made a vow years ago she'd somehow make a difference, that the friends she'd lost to reckless gunfire wouldn't have died in vain.

She felt lost herself at the moment, swirling in a sea of emotional confusion, and she didn't know which way to turn for help.

# Chapter Ten

"Now remember, Clifford, dear. You've promised to be an honorary co-chairman for our next big fund-raising event." Agatha swept past the squad room, her hand tucked through the D.A.'s arm as if she were like a debutante about to be presented. Her dress was a demure print with a lace collar and long sleeves. A bunch of silk violets added a touch of spring to a matching lace hat.

"You can count on me, Agatha. And my wife, too. She'll be delighted to serve on your arrangements committee. I'm sure of it."

"Lovely." Over her shoulder, Agatha said to the deputy police chief, who was chatting amiably with her attorney, "And you, Robert, dear, are going to recruit coaches for the sports programs at Chandler House."

"As many as you need," the chief agreed. "Our men—and women," he added when he caught sight of Sam in the hallway, "are always glad to have a chance to interact in a positive way with the gang community. It's a win-win situation for us all."

"Speaking of that," Agatha said, "perhaps we can

arrange for a baseball game between your officers and our All Stars. Wouldn't that be a wonderful event? The local community could get involved. I imagine the mothers could put together a potluck affair with ethnic dishes that would draw people from blocks around. What would you think about that?"

Jaw slack, Sam stared after the departing entourage. Aunt Agatha was being treated like no criminal she'd ever seen. More like a queen—or Robin Hood's grandmother, she thought with a wry smile. Clearly, the woman had a silver tongue—much like her favorite nephew.

Turning, Rogan's blue-eyed gaze snared her. Her heart missed a beat before it settled into a more regular rhythm.

Several seconds ticked by before she found her voice. "Your aunt appears to have charmed the upper echelon of our fair city's governmental officials. How did she manage to do that?"

"We were able to work out a restitution program. No one would benefit by Agatha being locked up."

Sam had always understood that and was pleased the powers-that-be realized it, too. "Does that mean you're personally going to have to make good on all the losses?" she guessed.

"Maybe." He shoved his hands into his trouser pockets. He looked tired, lines of strain etching the corners of his eyes and tilting his sensual lips downward. "Agatha may not have an elevator that quite reaches the top floor, but she is one smart woman. She suggested we quietly approach the victims she stole from. If they are willing to 'contribute' their jewelry to the cause, then nothing more will be said.

"On the other hand, if they want to be reimbursed for their losses, I'll do it, but anonymous stories just may be released to the papers, particularly the tabloids, that their parsimony may send a sweet, eighty-six-year-old do-gooder to jail. That seems like it would be a pretty persuasive argument."

Sam swallowed a laugh. "Good grief, that's blackmail!"

"I, for one, hope it works. There's a lot of money involved, Sam. According to her own records, my aunt's commitment to her charities knows no bounds."

He looked so weary, Sam wished she could hold him and offer him comfort. But she didn't have the right. By lying, she'd lost something terribly important to her, and she didn't know how to get it back.

"Look," she said, her own hands sliding self-consciously into her jacket pockets. "I'll need to pick up my car and things at your house. I can have somebody bring me over there tomorrow, if that would be convenient." She hated the formal sound of her request, a tone that gave no hint they had once—all too briefly—been lovers. Or that she wished they could be again.

His expression closed, he studied her for several seconds before he said, "You can come back with me tonight. Might as well get it over with."

In spite of herself, Sam's heart lurched. It was pretty obvious he wanted her gone from his life as soon as possible. Given the circumstances, and how she had lied to him, Sam could hardly object. But it still hurt. "Okay. Whenever you're ready to go."

ROGAN SHOVED open the door to his house.

Tail wagging, Goofus shot past him to greet Sam, licking her face, relishing the attention she gave him.

The stupid dog didn't know a thing about loyalty, Rogan decided, admittedly with a whole carload of sour grapes fermenting in his belly.

He'd wanted to protect Sam, to be a surrogate brother to her. Though he hadn't exactly acted in a brotherly fashion this past weekend, he conceded. But that didn't change the fact she had taken advantage of his good intentions.

He'd tried to rescue her, to find her a good husband.

In return, she'd moved into his house under false pretenses and damn well gotten under his skin the same way. If she'd had her way, he'd likely be in jail by now, neatly ambushed by a headful of copper curls and laughing green eyes, not to mention the sexiest body he'd ever come across—and a passionate nature, intelligence, and athletic grace that would rival any man's fantasies.

Except she was a cop!

So good at her job, she hadn't even needed his help to subdue an armed holdup man at that gas station.

Some useless big brother he was. But it didn't matter. She had betrayed him. Lied to him.

He remembered his father forcing him to lie to his mother about his infidelities, to betray her trust. He'd been fifteen that year—almost a man. It had made him feel small and dirty. He'd hated even the smallest falsehood ever since, unless it was to make a person feel better, not worse. And he'd never looked at his father in the same way.

Stepping into the entryway, his gaze slid to the throw rug on the floor. His body reacted with a fierce tautness as he remembered how they had made love there—the frantic way he had torn her clothes from her, his swift entry as she spread her legs, his climax, so powerful it had shattered all he had ever known or thought about sex before.

He'd never be able to walk into his house again without those images colliding with the lies she'd told him.

"It shouldn't take me long to pack. I didn't really have much with me."

Sam circled the edge of the throw rug, her gaze averted, and Rogan wondered if she was remembering that first time, too.

His groin muscles tightened. "There's no rush."

She paused at the foot of the steps. "I appreciate—"

"Let me know when you're packed. I'll help carry your bags out," he said as he walked through the house, opened the sliding-glass door and walked out onto the deck. Goofus followed Sam upstairs.

The sun was a red ball the color of Sam's hair, all fiery and bright, slipping into the sea. Whitecaps lifted by a stiff afternoon breeze dotted the ocean like curling quotation marks set against the gray expanse. The waves hummed in rapid succession, hurling themselves against the dark, wet sand on the beach, then raced back to hide in the next line of white foam.

A muscle ticked in Rogan's jaw.

Normally the sight that greeted him from his deck was soothing. Now it irritated the hell out of him and he wasn't quite sure why.

He stood there a long time, long enough for the sun to vanish, the sea to grow calm and the air to turn cool. Goofus reappeared. The unfaithful wretch lifted his paws to the top rail and gazed out to sea, his tail swiping an invisible path through the salt-flavored air.

Without looking, Rogan knew Sam was standing behind him at the open door.

"Why a cop?" he asked.

His question caught Sam off guard. "It's an honorable profession."

"So is being an engineer, or a telephone operator, or running a pizza parlor." He turned halfway toward her, his strong profile catching the light from inside the house. "Why police work?"

She supposed he deserved an answer, and perhaps it would help him understand why she'd felt it necessary to deceive him.

"I had two very close friends in high school," she said, joining him at the railing. She watched a breaker roll toward the shore in a curve of silver. "Marcia Bolten and Dee Stoneware. We were all on the volleyball team. We were all going to go to Cal Poly San Luis Obispo together. One afternoon we were standing on the lawn outside of school. I can't remember why we were in that particular spot at that exact instant, or what we were talking about. It was all so...innocuous."

Her voice faltered. She could remember a thousand other details—the sound of gunfire that she had at first thought was firecrackers. Screams—mostly hers. A carload of boys and squealing tires as they sped by. The sight of blood spreading across the green grass in a grotesque pattern of death.

"What is it, Sam?" Rogan's gentle voice erased the images from her mind.

She swallowed hard, steadying herself. "There was a drive-by shooting. Those things didn't happen at our school. We all thought the affluence of the neighborhood would keep us safe. It didn't."

"Your friends?"

"They both died. Marcia right away. Dee made it as far as the hospital."

"My God..." His hand covered hers on the railing where her knuckles had gone white. "I'm so sorry, Sam."

"I'd been standing right between them, Rogan. It was like they had been shot protecting me. The police never caught the shooters. As far as they could tell, Marcia and Dee were simply victims of a random act of violence. I was spared by the same haphazard chance."

"And you still feel guilty you survived."

She lifted her gaze to meet his. "I swore then I'd spend my life putting criminals behind bars where they couldn't hurt anyone else. A patrol officer is limited in what he or she can do. I took the undercover assignment because I thought it would eventually provide me with a leg up toward promotion, toward *real* police work. I want to catch those cretins who think they can get away with murder."

"And every time you arrest a thief or a murderer you're trying to even the score."

"Marcia's and Dee's deaths have to stand for something. I won't let their lives be meaningless. I *will* make a difference. It's the only way I can live with myself." In the face of a good many obstacles, she'd held on to that dream. She wasn't about to let go of it now.

"So you put your life on the line like you did with that gunman in Bakersfield."

"It's part of the job. And nothing…absolutely *nothing* is going to stand in the way of my giving meaning to those two deaths." Even if it meant Sam had to put up with being the odd man out when it came to police work, a cop who didn't quite fit in— and one who ended up with a broken heart in the process.

"There has to be some other—"

"My college major was police science. I entered the academy almost as soon as I graduated, I wanted that much to be a cop. The only other jobs I've had were summers as a counselor for the YMCA and coaching volleyball part-time. Police work is what I do."

Aware that what she was saying probably made little sense to Rogan, she slid her hand out from under his. "I'd better get going. You never know how bad the traffic will be."

She thought for minute he might ask her to stay. At the very least, the way his gaze had focused on her lips, she thought he would kiss her. Deep down she wanted him to.

Instead he said, "Drive safely."

As she drove away from Malibu, her vision blurred by tears she refused to shed, Sam knew she'd left a big chunk of her heart behind.

He wasn't the right man for her anyway, she told herself—a wealthy playboy with women falling at his feet. But somehow the reminder rang hollow and did nothing to ease the ache in her chest.

ADAM SHANKED HIS DRIVER into the rough and swore.

"Your game's off today," Rogan observed casually.

"You've got that damn straight. But I'm still up two strokes on you."

"It's usually ten by now." Placing his ball, Rogan took a couple of practice swings. "Something must be bothering you."

"It's Eileen. Would you believe she's actually got a *job?* Hell, she wouldn't have known which side to butter her toast on if I hadn't told her. What kind of work can a woman like that do?"

"Maybe you never gave her enough credit."

Adam snorted derisively. "If you and Agatha hadn't butted into my business, Eileen would still be at home where she belongs."

Rogan took his shot. The ball sailed straight down the fairway, landing just shy of the green with gratifying precision. A chip shot would have him on the green in two, making par a strong possibility. Not that Rogan cared much one way or the other.

"Why would you want Eileen back home?" he asked his brother as they dropped their clubs into the bags on the back of the cart. "You never gave her anything but grief while you were married."

"I know we had our differences, but I didn't expect her to actually leave me. I gave her everything she asked for, didn't I?"

"Except fidelity."

"Hey, I'm a ladies' man. What else can I say?"

Adam swung into the driver's seat. "She should have understood. Those other women never meant anything to me."

Rogan heard the echo of their father's words. "A recreational activity—like golf."

"Precisely."

The asphalt path led downhill from the seventeenth hole. Going too fast for the terrain, Adam nearly lost control of the cart on a sharp curve.

"What galls the hell out of me," Adam said, unconcerned by the near disaster, "is that Eileen needs me. She always has—and now she won't admit it."

"Evidently she doesn't need you as much as you thought."

"Well, she's not going to get a dime from me. Agatha's trying to get me to break our prenuptial agreement. No chance, I say. No woman's going to take me to the cleaners."

His brother had always thought women were motivated solely by money, and maybe some of them were. But that wasn't the case with Sam. She sure didn't need Rogan—not for his money or his connections. She was taking care of herself just fine. She'd even left the emerald necklace and earrings behind when she moved out. He'd meant them to be a gift.

But that didn't mean Rogan had stopped worrying about her. Lord knew what kind of trouble she was getting herself into as a cop. She had a reckless streak, he decided, that made her want to prove herself by taking too many risks. Instead, it would be easier for him to imagine her safely at home raising babies.

The picture of her raising *his* babies leapt into his

mind so swiftly he didn't have a chance to block the image.

"Damn," he muttered, swinging out of the cart when it came to a stop.

He'd hardly slept a wink since she'd moved out. The police scanner he'd bought hadn't helped much, particularly after he heard her voice responding to a call for backup to a robbery in progress—shots fired. She was on patrol again, and it scared the hell out of him.

Just because she didn't think she needed him to watch out for her, it didn't mean Rogan agreed. Though it still hurt like crazy that she had lied to him. People who care about each other shouldn't do that.

Adam hauled a club from his bag. "Let's get this game over with. I've got a date."

Rogan shot his brother a look. "You never learn, do you?" Even faced with the end of his marriage, Adam Prescott hadn't seen the value of fidelity. Clearly it was a case of bad genes.

Adam's lips canted into his famous lady-stopping grin. "Hey, little brother, there's a party at Marge Cummings's house Friday night. Now that your redheaded cop friend has moved out, how 'bout I fix you up with a date. I know a couple of hot little numbers who ought to be available. They'll show you a good time."

Rogan was less than enthusiastic. "I'll think about it."

Adam's iron-shot out of the rough landed right on the green, the ball rolled to the edge of the cup and fell in. "Keep your checkbook handy, little brother. You're still gonna owe me."

SAM CAUGHT the headlights in her rearview mirror for the third time. She was being followed.

The residential streets of Santa Monica were lightly traveled this time of night. Earlier she'd responded to a homicide call at a fast-food restaurant. That had been about dinner time. Now it was well past midnight. Before the detectives had shown up she'd gotten a decent description of the gunman but no license plate and no name. Now the investigation was in somebody else's hands. Tomorrow she'd be in a black-and-white again, patrolling the streets, and there'd be other cases. More violence. More frustration. And little way to truly make a difference.

She slowed, hoping to get a better look at the vehicle that was tailing her. Unfortunately he dropped back, too.

If she had to guess, she'd say it was some pervert who had spotted her traveling alone, or a guy planning a follow-home robbery. Though why he'd pick someone with an old Honda was beyond her.

Wouldn't he be surprised to discover she was a cop?

Though if she did this right, she'd avoid a confrontation altogether.

Turning onto her street, she rolled slowly past her duplex then accelerated and whipped into the alley that led to the garage. She pressed the button on the remote door opener. The door was still going up when she sped inside, slammed on her brakes, hit the device again and watched as the door closed behind her. Switching off the lights with one hand, she simultaneously killed the ignition with a flick of her other wrist.

Then she waited.

Moments later the flash of headlights swept across the small garage window, and she heard the hum of a vehicle cruising by.

Exhaling, she got out of the car. The mild surge of adrenaline she'd felt had her heart pumping a little faster than usual. She ordered herself to take another deep breath. No harm, no foul, she thought as she made her way into the house. The whole thing could have been a coincidence.

Without turning on any lights, she made her way to the front window, just to make sure. She pulled back the curtain.

Adrenaline flooded through her system; her palms went clammy and her heartbeat kicked up again.

A man was standing in the shadow of a tree across the street. She couldn't make out his features but she had the distinct feeling he was watching the duplex.

*Watching her.*

She ducked back from the window. For another woman it would have been reasonable to call the police to check it out. For Sam that would mean a lot of razzing from the guys. She could do without that.

Slipping out the back again, she jogged down the alley and around to the front. Overhanging trees cast dark shadows along the sidewalk that the streetlights couldn't penetrate; dangerous shadows that also provided her with enough cover to approach the man without being seen.

He was so intent on watching her duplex he didn't hear her coming. Oddly, she thought he looked vaguely familiar.

Using both hands, she leveled her weapon at him from a few feet away.

"Police. I want your hands up, fingers locked on top of your head. Now."

## Chapter Eleven

The man's head whipped around and his hands shot up. "It's me, Sam. Don't shoot."

Slowly, she lowered her weapon. "Rogan? What on earth are you doing here?" He was wearing a dark suit and his tie was loose at the collar. His hair looked rumpled, as though he'd run his fingers through the strands a thousand times, futilely trying to comb them into some semblance of order...and failing dismally.

"I, uh, I wanted to make sure you got home safely."

"You followed me home from the station?"

He looked at her sheepishly. "This isn't a real good neighborhood, you know. Things can happen to a woman alone."

"Oh, for pity's sake! I'm a police officer. I can take care of myself."

"Sure. I know that. I just thought—"

"You're crazy, that's what you are. I thought you were a follow-home robber. If you'd made any kind of false move, I could have shot you. Or one of the other neighbors could have spotted you sneaking around and called the police. How would you have explained yourself then?''

He shrugged. ''Can I put my hands down now?''

''Oh, of course.'' As she holstered her gun, Sam didn't know whether to laugh or cry. In spite of her best intentions, she'd missed Rogan terribly. She wanted to hug and kiss him, and at the same time knew it would be the epitome of foolishness if she did.

''So, how's it going in the police business?''

Odd question, she mused. ''Fine, I guess. I'm back on patrol again.''

''That's kind of dangerous, isn't it?''

''I suppose it can be. But that's what cops get paid for, right?''

He shrugged again, this time putting his hands in his pockets.

A porch light flicked on behind them. Sam glanced over her shoulder. Apparently their voices had disturbed the neighbors.

''Look, it's the middle of the night. Not exactly a good time to be standing on the sidewalk having a conversation,'' she said. In spite of the late hour, Sam didn't feel in the least sleepy. Her unit had been called to the scene of a murder, where she'd strung the yellow police tape and kept curious spectators out of the crime scene—earning a big chunk of overtime as the hours sped by. Combined with Rogan scaring the wits out of her, adrenaline was still flowing through her veins. She wouldn't be able to get to sleep for hours.

''You want to come in for a few minutes?'' she asked. It was a stupid idea. She knew that as soon as the words were out of her mouth. But as if her mouth had no connection to her good sense, she added, "I think I've got a couple of beers in the refrigerator." In a perfect world, he would have declined and that would have made up for Sam's reckless invitation.

"Sounds good to me."

As they walked to her front door, she was acutely conscious of Rogan beside her, the late hour, and what the wakeful neighbors were no doubt thinking— a late date between lovers. But it wasn't like that. It couldn't be, not when she had lied to him and he must surely hate her for that.

Except he was here, checking on her to make sure she got home safely.

Darn peculiar behavior for a man who should still be mad at her.

That thought gave her an equally odd feeling in her midsection, sort of warm and achy. She didn't dare hope they could start over. She still had enough sense to know she couldn't count on a long term commitment from a millionaire playboy. After all, the housekeeper's daughter had seen the Prescott family firsthand. She knew what she was up against.

Once inside her duplex, she switched on the light. "Make yourself comfortable. I'll get the beer."

Instead of sitting, Rogan made a slow turn of the modestly sized living room. He had never been inside Sam's home—no closer than the front walkway. There were lots of feminine touches—a windowsill crammed with houseplants, everyone of them looking healthy and well cared for. Though not expensive, the furniture was tasteful, the colors subdued except for bright splashes of pink and green pillows and a matching valance above otherwise bland windows.

The few knickknacks on tables or tucked into book-shelves had been selected with equal care for quality, not extravagance.

Most of all, he could catch her faint scent in the room, as fresh as the plants but far more erotic. He felt like a man addicted. He simply hadn't been able to stay away.

"Here you go." Sam came back into the room, two bottles in hand. "It's a light. I hope you don't mind."

"Perfect. I probably need to cut down my calories anyway."

Sam didn't think so, given his athletic physique, but she let the comment slide. "You need a glass?"

"No, this is fine." He lifted the bottle in salute, then took a swig.

She watched in fascination as his Adam's apple moved. His evening whiskers, at this late hour, were quite dark; his cheeks appeared drawn as though he hadn't been sleeping well or eating regularly. Neither had she, if anyone should care to ask.

She felt awkward, like an adolescent on her first date.

"So how's Aunt Agatha and all of her cohorts?"

His lips slid into a grin and, like magic, a dimple creased his cheek. "Busier than ever, if that's possible. Now that the cash flow has slowed at Chandler House she feels like she has to work twice as hard for fear they might have to lay off some of the staff. I swear she could squeeze dollar bills from a turnip."

"She's an amazing woman." Using some small amount of caution, Sam sat in a straight-back chair near the bookcase. She'd changed out of her uniform and had slipped into more comfortable slacks and a silk blouse. Ready to relax with her late evening date, she thought wryly.

Rogan chose the couch. He leaned back, crossing one ankle over the other, the fact that he'd neglected to put on socks now obvious. Though he wasn't a particularly large man, he still seemed to fill the room. Or maybe it was simply his subtly commanding presence that occupied every inch of the space.

Desperately, Sam struggled to suppress the images of those two short days during which they had been lovers. It wasn't easy.

"Agatha's also twisting Adam's arm about his prenuptial agreement. She feels like Eileen deserves support *and* half the estate. Agatha is threatening to lead a stockholders' rebellion if he doesn't cooperate."

Sam grinned. "She's a woman after my own heart." Though admittedly a large chunk of Sam's heart already belonged to Rogan. Not that he appeared to want it, at least not on a permanent basis.

They talked in fits and starts in the quiet of the predawn hours, each one obviously having trouble finding a comfortable topic. Friends or lovers, their relationship was hard to define.

Finally they'd run out of both beer and conversation.

Rogan stood. "I guess I'd better let you get some sleep. You must have to get up early."

"You're right." Less than four hours from now.

He walked to the door and she followed him. He turned abruptly, causing them to collide.

Sam drew in a quick breath.

"Sorry," he mumbled. Automatically his hands went to her shoulders to steady her.

"No problem." Except she was drowning in the blue depths of his eyes, wanting him so badly it hurt and knowing that was a damn fool thing to want.

"Maybe I'll drop by again, if that's okay."

"Sure. But don't sneak up on me. Some of us macho cops have itchy trigger fingers." His gaze focused on her lips, and Sam knew the itch she wanted scratched wasn't anywhere near her finger.

"You'll be careful, won't you?" His voice was low and husky, full of an intimacy that Sam didn't dare encourage—not if she wanted to keep the remaining pieces of her heart intact.

"That's how I've been trained."

He lowered his head toward hers.

A battle of good sense versus unbridled desire raged inside her. With considerable effort, reason won. She placed her palms on his unyielding chest. His heart beat hard, the rhythm as irregular as her own. "Good night, Rogan."

He cleared his throat. His hands dropped to his side. "Good night, Carrot Top. Sleep tight." He reached for the doorknob.

Sam's legs were weak with wanting, her throat tight with emotion. No question about it, she was the world's worst fool, her need was too powerful to resist. She *couldn't* let him walk out that door.

"Rogan?" Her voice cracked.

He turned and she was in his arms. He covered her face with kisses, a hot trail that started at her temple and moved quickly to that sensitive spot below her ear. His breath was warm and sweet. As his fingers stroked her neck beneath her collar, his lips nipped closer and closer to her mouth.

His name became little more than a moan on her lips. She plowed her fingers through the hair at his nape, the fine strands capturing her, ensnaring her.

"Seems to me I've been forgetting something when it came to making love with you." His tongue traced the shape of her lips.

"Hmm. I don't recall any major omissions."

"Things happened so fast, I forgot the seduction part."

"Seduction? I don't think—" In fact she wasn't able to think at all, not after he claimed her mouth in a deep kiss like none she'd ever experienced before— even with him. He toyed with her slowly, teasing with languid strokes that sent wave after wave of liquid heat to her arms and chest, and to her belly, where it curled in on itself.

Her body boneless, she floated on a sea of sensual pleasure. Her breasts felt heavy, her womanhood moist and ready. Yet still he played with her, as though he'd be content to investigate her mouth for hours on end.

Where before they had come together in one explosive consummation after another, even while they were on the yacht, now he appeared determined to savor each moment.

His forearm brushed against her breast, almost accidentally, as he altered their positions, angling his tongue deeper. Her breath caught, she tasted him, and she exhaled, mixing their shared air in a shudder that rippled to every one of her nerve endings. His fingertips skimmed her cheek in an extraordinarily tender caress that brought tears to her eyes.

"Rogan," she sobbed. Her fingers flexed into his shoulders.

"Shh, Carrot Top. We've got lots of time." He lifted his head to study her face. Her sweet flush of arousal made her beautiful; her parted lips, glistening and already softly swollen, waited for his next kiss. Her eyes pleaded with him in a mixture of need and confusion. An unfamiliar feeling that went well beyond sex slid through him. It was as though he had found a secret that had eluded him all of his life, but before he could give it a name, it was gone in the press of her body against his.

"Ah, Sam, you taste so good."

"The bedroom. Please."

"Absolutely." He scooped her up into his arms. Though his control was near the breaking point, he wanted to give her all the pleasure she deserved.

A lamp on the bedside table cast a golden glow in a room filled with florals and frills, a feminine room, a soft room that invited and tempted, just as Sam did when he placed her on the bed. He took great satisfaction in unbuttoning her blouse one button at a time, revealing her creamy skin, discovering the lacy edge of her bra. He explored there momentarily with his tongue before moving on.

He slipped her blouse from her shoulders, then lowered the strap. "Have I mentioned that you're beautiful?"

Sam couldn't remember. It didn't matter because his tenderness spoke with more potency than words could possibly convey. She could feel him everywhere. Touching. Caressing. Kissing. His fingers slipped beneath the waistband of her pants. She bucked and called his name, arching up to him. He delved deeper, and staggering pleasure whipped through her. Her body convulsed until she thought there was nothing left of her, in her.

And then he stripped the rest of her clothes away, filled her, until the blood pounded in her ears again and sensations pulsed through her in unending waves. Her vision blurred. His blue-black eyes gazed down at her just before he claimed her mouth again and they leapt together to a point beyond knowing.

SHE CAUGHT HERSELF whistling the next morning as she went into roll call.

Well, why not? she thought as she poured herself a cup of coffee. A woman had a right to be cheerful, didn't she? A woman in love, that is.

It was okay to feel like the sun was a little brighter today than it had ever been before, and her footsteps a little lighter. Strange she'd never realized being in love was a natural high. But then this was a first for her. If she could bottle the feeling, all the junkies in town would be out of business. And she'd be a millionaire.

Grinning so broadly it hurt her cheeks, she settled into a chair at the back of the room.

Garcia strode in almost immediately, the road map of wrinkles on his face drawn taut. "Sterling! Listen up."

Sam's good mood lost a good deal of its buoyancy. "Yes, sir?"

"You're back on loan to me. The Westside jewel thief struck again last night."

She stared at him incredulously. Could Aunt Agatha have reverted to her old tricks? "That's not possible," she said aloud, although she'd intended to keep her thoughts to herself.

Garcia cocked an eyebrow. "Yeah? Well I'll tell the victim you said that. I'm sure she'll be glad to hear such a clever bit of wisdom from a patrol officer."

A couple of the other guys in the room snickered.

"I didn't actually mean—"

"She lost a diamond brooch. Worth maybe three thou. Penny-ante compared to the rest of the stuff that's been lifted."

Thoroughly chastised, Sam asked, "Is it a copycat, do you think?"

"Don't know." He shoved a couple of sheets of paper at her. "This is the guest list Marjorie Cummings provided. I want you to interview her. Starting right now, your priority is the thefts, Sterling. Given the way the boys upstairs handled that Agatha Prescott woman, the chief's name and the D.A.'s will both be mud if we don't put a stop to whoever has sticky fingers. Permanently."

She scanned the list, her stomach sinking with each name she read. Agatha's was there. So was Rogan's as well as most of his society friends. She felt a terrible sense of dread. This time an arrest would be made. She could only pray it wouldn't be someone close to Rogan.

SHE DIDN'T LEARN MUCH from interviewing Marjorie Cummings, except the description of the stolen brooch. Sam's next stop was Rogan's house. She dreaded telling him he was back on a suspect list—and she was the investigating officer. Maybe when he saw her in uniform, he'd catch on that this was not a social call.

His welcoming smile, the familiar, endearing cant of his lips, nearly melted her insides. "Didn't expect to see you until tonight, sweetheart. Can't say I'm sorry, though."

Before she could object, he'd pulled her into his arms and was kissing her. Deeply. Thoroughly. As he had last night, or rather early this morning.

Vaguely she was aware of Goofus rubbing up against her—and the fact that this was no way for an investigating police officer to be acting.

"Wait, Rogan. We can't do this." She shoved at his chest.

"Hmm. I think we do it very well. Though it's gotta be the first time I've ever kissed a cop—in uniform."

"No, you don't understand." She ducked away from him and stepped into the house, nearly falling over Goofus in the process. "I'm here on official business."

"Official? What are you talking about?"

"There was another robbery last night. A diamond brooch."

He tensed, shoulders going rigid. "What's that got to do with me?"

"I have to question you."

His forehead furrowed and his eyes narrowed. "Don't you know by now that I'm no thief?"

"Of course I do, Rogan." At least her heart told her that was true. "But this is my job. You were on the invitation list."

He whirled and marched into the house. Closing the door behind him, Sam followed. *Please don't let him lie to me.*

"You know damn well where I was last night. How can you even ask?"

Heartsick, she pulled out a notepad. "Marjorie Cummings said you were at the party. She didn't remember precisely when you arrived or when you left." Or who he'd been with, if anyone. But Rogan had evaded answering her—the same thing as a lie.

He stopped at the dining table, his fingers curling over the back of a chair. He was wearing his usual cut-offs and a gray T-shirt with the sleeves ripped out.

"All right, I was there. I arrived about nine-thirty, stayed a couple of hours and left. Is that what you wanted to know?"

Her hand shook as she noted the times he'd mentioned on her notepad. The brooch had been missed shortly after midnight. "Were you with anyone?"

Silent seconds spun out like fragile threads of trust that could be easily broken. Beyond where Rogan was standing, the ocean glistened silver in the morning sun. Sam knew she'd foolishly risked her heart and now she'd pay the price.

He turned, the blue of his eyes somehow bleak as he spoke. "I had a date."

Her throat felt tight. "What was her name?"

"You'd moved out. It's not like we had an understanding or anything."

"Her name?"

"I took her home early. I was worried about you. You're so damn determined to prove you're a good cop, I was afraid you were risking your neck somewhere."

She simply gazed at Rogan, waiting for him to answer the question she'd asked, and felt like her insides were shattering into a thousand pieces.

"Ah, hell! Her name was Heidi."

She wrote that down, though her vision blurred and she had to blink twice before she could see clearly. She had a job to do, one that didn't allow her to show how much he had hurt her. "Does she have a last name?"

"I don't know. Schmidt. Schmiddling. Something like that."

"Do you have her address?"

In two long strides, he crossed the room to her. He framed her face with his big hands and held her so she couldn't look away. "Don't crucify me with this, Sam. I had a date with a woman I didn't know and didn't much enjoy. Then I ended up at your place because I was sick with worry. We made love, which I did enjoy. And so did you."

"Yes." Her weak reply was hardly professional. "But you weren't going to tell me, were you? If I hadn't learned from Ms. Cummings you were there, you would have kept quiet. That's the same as lying, Rogan." An act she couldn't tolerate, and a wake-up call that Prescott men often did just that. Rogan's father certainly had lied often to his wife; son Adam was cut from the same cloth. She'd hoped—evidently futilely—that Rogan was different.

"I didn't want to upset you."

"Somewhere along the way I learned honesty is the best policy."

"Except when you're playing undercover cop."

Guilt pricked her. "Exception granted."

"I'm not a thief, Sam."

He still didn't get it. His honesty in their relationship was far more important to her than whether or not he was a thief. Her love was deep enough, enduring enough, that she'd be willing to wait for him outside the prison walls, if that's what was required. In the same way, she didn't care an iota for how much money he had. She'd rather he'd made his living with his hands—a bricklayer or starving artist, it didn't matter. If he were faithful to her, she would be confident she could give him her heart for safekeeping.

But she didn't think he understood that. Oddly, she supposed her father had never understood how devastating his desertion had been to her, either. Maybe men were biologically incapable of such obvious insights into the female mind...and heart.

"If you can find Heidi's address, I'd appreciate it. I'll have to interview her, along with the other people who attended the party."

He swore long and softly. "I'm going with you."

"You can't do that."

"Why the hell not?"

"Because it's police business."

"You're *my* business, Carrot Top. And I'm not going to let you out of my sight. I have a vested interest in your investigation. One way or another, I'm going to prove to you I'm not a thief."

That might well be true. But could he also prove he was worthy of her love?

# Chapter Twelve

Sam drove the nondescript police-issue sedan with authority, just like everything else she did. Another of her many attributes Rogan admired.

Until last night he hadn't realized how much he'd come to respect her. It had been a revelation.

His date with curvaceous young Heidi Schmidt...or Schmiddling...had been a mistake. While she was sweet enough, he supposed, Sam had an attractive maturity that went well beyond her years, yet she was still fun to be with. Sam had a carefully toned body he could admire, not just flashy curves created mostly by a push-up bra. Sam was intelligent, genuinely cared about others and in no way could she be considered a phony.

Besides, he'd spent the whole evening worrying about Sam. Then, when he'd gone to her house, he hadn't found her at home. Panic reared its ugly head. So he'd gone to the police station, asked around and eventually followed her home. He hadn't been able to tear himself away.

When they made love, the intensity of her response made him forget who he was. He'd had images of a house with a white picket fence, kids playing on swings and days together at the beach, Sam waiting for him when he got home from a normal kind of job. A picture of permanence. *Of forever.*

She'd made him want that kind of life.

But with one blind date, he'd proved what both he and Sam had known all along. Forever wasn't a part of his genetic code.

He wished to God he hadn't listened to his "ladies' man" brother just this once.

Now he didn't know how to undo that slip, or even if he could in her eyes. For the first time in his life, he wanted to perform surgery on the Prescott DNA.

In return, Sam had reverted to form and suspected he was a diamond thief. And if not him, one of his friends or family members.

Why couldn't he have fallen for a woman who was empty-headed? A woman who'd be stupid enough to put up with a Prescott?

She wheeled into the circular drive at Aunt Agatha's house and came to a stop in front of the brick walkway.

"How well do you know Marjorie Cummings?" she asked, all business, a uniformed cop at work.

He shrugged. "She's made her living by marrying very wealthy men, divorcing them and banking the proceeds. Three times now, I think. Maybe more. In between, she encourages men to give her pretty little baubles to keep her happy. She's sufficiently charming that she's developed a very lucrative business and has a good many admirers."

Cringing from that kind of life-style, Sam's throat was still tight with the knowledge Rogan might be a party to the theft—or knew someone who was. She forced herself to ask, "Were you one of her admirers?"

"Hell, no! I like her well enough but not the way you're suggesting."

"No baubles?"

"None." A muscle flexed at the sharp angle of his jaw.

Sam wanted to feel relieved by his denial but her nerves were so on edge she wasn't sure what to believe. She had a crime to solve. In spite of everything, of the boredom and frustration she'd found on the job, she still wanted to be a cop. She couldn't let her emotions—her futile dreams of being with Rogan—interfere with whatever facts she was able to elicit.

Some sixth sense compelled her to probe further with a question she suspected Rogan wouldn't like any better than he had the first. "How about your brother Adam?"

He popped the door open on the passenger side. "Adam gets around but he doesn't give me the details. Frankly, I'm not interested."

"I see," she replied tautly, exiting the car. In many respects, the brothers appeared to be total opposites. Yet she couldn't quite believe Rogan, with all the women who were at his beck and call, had entirely eschewed the life-style of the rich and famous. Even when he was an adolescent she'd seen him with a covey of beauties throwing themselves at his feet. His by-the-beach casual life-style was hardly a model for the perfect mate. She shouldn't have given what little remained of her heart into the hands of a man she wasn't convinced would value it.

She and Rogan walked up the path and Juanita admitted them to the house, her aging smile beatific—and *knowing*—as she glanced at the two of them together. "The missus is in the garden room. She will be pleased to see you—both of you."

"Aunt Agatha is a confirmed matchmaker and so is Juanita," Rogan said under his breath as they walked through the foyer and into the garden room. "They've both been trying to get me married off for years."

And they'd failed, Sam noted, not sure how she should feel about that.

"Rogan, dear. And Samantha. What a lovely surprise! And don't you look charming in your uniform, dear. Blue is definitely your color. Of course, so is green." From her seat in a white wicker chair, Agatha raised her arms to grant Rogan a hug, turning her cheek for a dutiful kiss. She wore a long, flowing hostess gown in a shocking shade of violet matched by the brilliant satin turban wrapped around her head. Apparently she'd been doing paperwork because there were sheets of ledger paper filling her lap.

"Sam thinks you've been up to mischief again," Rogan said without preamble.

A flush raced to Sam's cheeks. "That's not true. I just need to ask a few—"

"Whatever is wrong, dear?"

Pale blue eyes lifted innocently to meet Sam's—which didn't mean much with a woman who'd stolen thousands upon thousands of dollars of jewelry over the last few years. Sam staunchly reminded herself of that.

She pulled her notepad and pencil from her pocket.

"You were at Marjorie Cummings's party last night?"

"Oh, yes, it was a quiet little affair. But Marjorie is such a charming young lady and she has, in her own way, been generous to Chandler House. It was kind of her to invite me."

"Were you asking her for an additional contribution?"

"Dammit, Sam," Rogan blurted. "Don't beat around the bush. Ask Agatha if she stole Marge's brooch."

Agatha paled.

"Rogan, this is my investigation. I don't want you interfer—"

"And Agatha is my family." Protectively taking his aunt's hand, Rogan glowered at Sam.

The fragile twining threads of love and trust Sam had felt for Rogan last night began to shred.

"Children, please." Rising, Agatha took Sam's hand and placed it over Rogan's. "You two mustn't fight over me. I love you both, truly I do. In no way would I want to come between you."

"If she can't trust me and my family, there's nothing to come between," Rogan groused.

Sam struggled to remember who and what she was—a cop—and why she was here. The feel of Rogan's hand beneath hers was far too familiar, his masculine scent too freshly a part of her memory not to react to his closeness. Perhaps if he'd changed out of his cutoffs, if he didn't still smell of the salty ocean that was his neighbor, it might have been easier for Sam to establish a more forceful police persona. Instead, her knees took on that habitual weakness that overcame her whenever Rogan touched her.

Determinedly, she withdrew her hand. "I'm not singling out your family, Rogan. I have to question everyone who was involved." She turned to his aunt. "Do you recall what time you left the party, Agatha?"

"Oh, my, let me see. Alfred had arranged a lovely buffet table. There're so many fresh fruits this time of year, you know, and I—"

"Alfred?"

"The caterer, dear. Everyone uses him for their little affairs. He's so thorough, you know."

"I see." Sam jotted the name down on her pad, the image of a waiter with protruding eyes and a small tattoo on his hand coming to mind. She'd have to check out the caterer's list of employees. "Go ahead. You were saying what time you left."

"Shortly after I finished eating, I believe. Perhaps eleven. I've been a little weary of late." The lines on her face shifted with a self-deprecating smile. "I hate to admit it, but it may be my age is catching up with me."

"Not likely, Aunt Agatha," Rogan insisted. "You can still run rings around anyone half your age. Me included."

"Thank you, dear boy. Isn't he sweet?" she said to Sam. "He'd be a wonderful catch for the right woman, don't you think?"

Without intending to, Sam met Rogan's gaze. Her heart squeezed and her mouth went dry. Whatever else he might be, Rogan Prescott was definitely a heartbreaker.

"Yes, well…" She forced her thoughts back to the case. "About Marjorie Cummings, did you notice her wearing a diamond brooch with a circle of small rubies?"

"Let me think. I've been so distracted lately about Chandler House. The board of directors is actually considering laying off the executive director. Such a pity, but our funds are so short, you know, now that I can't contribute as much as I used to."

By stealing and cashing in the jewels, Sam recalled all too clearly.

"Oh, hello there, you two. I didn't know we had company."

Sam turned at the sound of Eileen's voice. The young woman was decked out in a stunning bright pink silk suit, her blond hair swept up in an elegant do. As she crossed the room with a sway that mimicked a fashion model on a runway, Sam's gaze focused on the distinctive brooch fastened to Eileen's lapel.

Rogan met Eileen halfway. "How's the job?" he asked, giving her a quick kiss on the cheek.

"Wonderful. Everyone's been so kind to me. I should have gone to work years ago." Her smile and body language were far more confident than the night she'd been arrested, or even during those days she'd spent at Rogan's house. Now she held her head high, as though she were quite pleased with herself. "In fact, I'm on my way out to lunch at the country club with some friends to celebrate my first paycheck."

"That's terrific." Rogan gave her an encouraging thumbs up.

Sam had another topic on her mind. "Eileen, I

can't help but notice the pin you're wearing." One that rather closely matched the description of the stolen brooch. "It's lovely."

Eileen's smile took on a cat-who-ate-the-canary slant. "Thank you."

"Were you by chance at Marjorie Cummings's party last night?" She hadn't been on the guest list, but possibly—

"Oh, no. I knew Adam would be there and well... That would have been far too awkward."

"Sam, what are you getting at now?" Rogan demanded to know.

Agatha admonished her nephew. "Don't be rude, dear boy. Sam's simply curious."

"I only wondered how long Eileen has had that particular brooch. It's so striking."

Smiling, Eileen glanced at the pin. "It came by special messenger this morning."

"Special messenger?" Sam practically leapt into the air and clicked her heels together. "Who sent it?"

"I don't know. There was no note with it. A secret admirer, I suppose you could say."

"But you must have some idea."

Eileen looked shyly away. "I haven't been accepting Adam's phone calls. I can't be sure, of course, but I assume... There really wouldn't be anyone else."

*Adam!* Sam all but shouted his name. Of course. The two-timing, womanizing scoundrel...and thief! As soon as she could locate the package and identify the messenger service and the sender, she was going to have this case wrapped up. So much for the final chapter in the Westside jewel theft case.

She could hardly wait to snap the cuffs on Adam Prescott. He deserved to be locked up for what he'd done to Eileen—and a lot of other women, she imagined.

She tried not to think about how Rogan would feel when she broke the news to him that his brother was probably going to jail for a very long time.

"YOU'RE OUT of your mind!"

"Not likely." Sam strode out the front door of Agatha's house toward her car, Rogan keeping pace.

"Why would Adam steal Marge's pin and send it to Eileen? That's ridiculous."

"According to Marjorie, Adam was the one who gave it to her in the first place, a couple of years ago."

"It makes no sense that Adam would take back a gift he'd given to a woman he'd been having a…well, an affair with and then give it to his wife, who is about to divorce him."

"Maybe he was feeling guilty about his affairs."

"Adam? The original ladies' man? My brother's sense of guilt shriveled like a prune as soon as he hit puberty."

Before unlocking the door, she locked onto Rogan's gaze over the top of the car. "Do all the Prescott men have the same attitude about fidelity?"

He didn't flinch. "It's in the genes."

Sam felt like she'd been sucker punched. She'd desperately hoped for a different answer. She'd wanted to hear that faithlessness in marriage might be true for the other men in his family but not for Rogan.

Instead he'd all but admitted he was made from the same mold.

She believed him. She had to. There'd be no reason for him to lie—not about this.

Sick to her stomach, she got into the car just as her cell phone rang.

She pulled the instrument from the overhead visor and snapped it open. "Yes."

"Listen up! There's been another theft," Garcia announced without bothering to identify himself, not that his gravelly voice needed any introduction.

"Another one?" Good grief, what was going on? They appeared to have an epidemic on their hands.

"A diamond bracelet took wings this morning. A Pamela Morrison reported it missing after she had breakfast with Adam Prescott."

She shot a glance at Rogan. "I've recovered the brooch. It looks like Prescott was involved in that theft, too."

"Interesting. Maybe I had the wrong brother pegged."

Rogan's only crime appeared to be having relatives who succumbed too easily to temptation. "I have to check a delivery service before I can be sure," she warned the detective.

"Okay. But I want this thing resolved in a hurry."

So do I, she thought as she hung up.

She turned to Rogan. "Do you know Pamela Morrison?"

He shrugged. "Slightly. It's likely Adam knows her somewhat better."

"Very likely. He's been busy this morning snatching a diamond bracelet from her."

"I don't believe you." He snapped his seat belt in place when Sam started the car.

"We'll see."

"You're barking up the wrong tree," Rogan assured her as she pulled out of Agatha's driveway. "Adam might cheat the IRS, and he'd sure pull any fast one he could to get a supplier to cut his prices. But he wouldn't steal from his own mistresses."

"I gather you admire his keen sense of ethics."

"No, I don't." Folding his arms, he glared out the window.

He had a wonderfully strong profile, a straight nose and firm jaw. Sam's fingers itched with the tactile memory of how she had caressed his face last night. And kissed him. It wasn't fair that every detail about Rogan should be etched in her mind with such clarity. A woman ought to be able to forget things that hurt so much.

She swallowed the painful lump that filled her throat. "You were a little too quick to defend Aunt Agatha," she noted. "You were wrong about her. Now you're defending Adam the same way, with your head stuck in the sand."

"They may not be perfect, but they're family. That's good enough for me."

Sam wondered at his misplaced loyalty.

As she turned left onto the boulevard, she noticed a messenger service van turning into the street she'd just exited. It wasn't the messenger service she was en route to question. But it did strike her as an odd coincidence that two special deliveries would arrive within hours of each other in the same upscale residential neighborhood.

HER INVESTIGATION of the messenger service that had delivered the brooch to Eileen turned up absolutely no information of value. The transaction had been completed anonymously, so carefully it was impossible to track where the brooch had come from.

Someone had gone to a great deal of trouble to hide his identity. Understandably, Sam supposed, considering they were dealing with stolen property. It made her suspect Adam Prescott all the more. In spite of his wealth, a man of his standing in the community wouldn't want to get caught stealing gifts back from his assorted mistresses. If nothing else, it would cramp his style when he decided to move on to the next woman.

The fact that Rogan continued to stubbornly defend his brother made it all the more clear that they did not share the same set of values.

They arrived at the police station at midafternoon. Sam was hot, tired, and thoroughly discouraged about her personal life. She wasn't all that thrilled about the progress of the case, either, until she walked into the squad room.

Garcia swiveled around in his chair to face them. "We just picked up Adam Prescott. They're putting him in an interrogation room now."

"That's ridiculous!" Rogan bellowed. It was all he could do not to personally wipe that smug smile off the detective's face. For the better part of the day he'd put up with Sam's accusations against his brother. His patience had been strained to the limit.

"There was another robbery, Mr. Prescott. A lovely young woman named..." Garcia shuffled a few papers around on his cluttered desk. "Maddie

Burke is her name. She reported a pair of diamond earrings missing right after she had lunch with your brother at her home today. I'd say there was a lot of room for suspicion, what with three robberies all in one day, *all* of them connected to your brother.''

Rogan got in the detective's face, getting a powerful whiff of onions in the process. "*Now listen up,* buddy. My brother didn't steal that jewelry. He wouldn't do that.''

"Is this Maddie person one of his mistresses?" Sam asked.

He didn't look in her direction. He didn't want to admit the truth. "It doesn't matter. Something else is going on here. Adam isn't guilty and I demand the right to talk to him.''

Garcia's eyes narrowed. "You don't have any rights, Prescott. At this point, you're not a suspect. Your brother is.''

"You had me talk to Martin when you had him locked up.''

"It served my purposes then. *Now* it doesn't.''

"Then I want you to get Adam an attorney.''

"He hasn't asked for one.''

"Well, dammit! Get him one anyway!" Frustration knotted in Rogan's stomach. He might not like all the things his brother did—certainly not the way he treated women—but that didn't mean he was going to stand by and let them hang his brother on some trumped-up charge.

He whirled, glared at Sam, and marched away. He knew where the interrogation rooms were. He'd find Adam and tell him not to say one single damn syllable until he could get an attorney here for him. Then they'd sue the pants off the L.A.P.D. for false arrest.

Sam started to follow Rogan, to stop him from doing something that would get him in serious trouble. But Garcia's low warning of "Let him go" brought her to a halt. She shot the detective a questioning look.

"We'll let 'em talk a little and see what happens. If I know anything about human behavior, Adam will spill his guts to his little brother. And *we'll* get it all on tape."

Sam knew having an open mike in an interrogation room was standard procedure and perfectly legal, particularly when the suspect hadn't yet requested an attorney. On some level, she might question the department's ethics, but the fact was bad guys lied to the cops all the time. Somehow the thin blue line needed to come up with an edge.

Standing, Garcia said, "Let's go eavesdrop. You're gonna love it."

Sam didn't think so. She suspected when Rogan found out, he'd like it even less.

"THEY'RE CRAZY, Rogan," Adam was saying as Sam and Garcia arrived in the observation room, shielded by the two-way mirror. "Why on earth would I take back my gifts to Marge and the others? They're all charming ladies. They earned every penny I spent on them."

"Sam thinks you developed a bad case of guilt and wanted to make amends to Eileen."

"My, my, she is naive, isn't she? I'm troubled that Eileen actually left me, that's true. I didn't think she'd have the courage. But I'm sure, in time, she will become more reasonable. I'd hardly wish to set a precedence by *bribing* her with second-hand gifts. She'll come 'round on her own. Trust me on this, little brother. I haven't lost my touch with women.''

Sam's fingers balled into fists. She had a huge desire to shove Adam's smile right down his throat. The man was impossible!

''At least don't say a word until I can get your attorney here,'' Rogan said.

''Don't be silly. This whole affair is nonsense. All I need do is tell the truth.''

''Maddie told them you took her earrings when you had lunch with her today.''

''Lunch?'' Adam's eyes widened. ''I haven't seen Maddie in, well, it must be months. She's a dear girl, but a little demanding, if you know what I mean.''

''And Pamela. They said you had breakfast—''

''After the party last night? Are you serious? I took Stephanie home with me. It wasn't the most fascinating evening I've ever spent, but I assure you, she didn't leave until almost noon. I'd hardly have an opportunity to have breakfast with Pam.''

Garcia swore long and hard and very succinctly. If Sam hadn't been around the squad room for a long time, she would have blushed. As it was, she shared his views.

''He's not lying, is he?'' she said, almost rhetorically.

''Not a chance.'' Garcia's heavily lined face shifted into an expression of disgust. ''Get those women in here. Put 'em in the same room together and let 'em talk. Rogan's right. There's something very fishy going on and those wealthy broads are gonna learn I don't like to be conned.''

"Yes, sir."

"And throw that Rogan character out of the station. Send him home in a cab. I don't want him around when we question the women."

"Should I take him—"

"No. This is your case, Sterling. If those women don't talk on their own, you're gonna get 'em to tell you the truth. Woman to woman. Now, get hopping."

AT THE KNOCK on Rogan's door, he took another swig of his beer. He'd been waiting for hours. He'd known she'd come. Sometime.

And he'd known, whatever she said, that he couldn't avoid what needed to be done. He wasn't a forever kind of guy. If he asked Sam to give him a try, he'd be condemning her to eventual misery. He couldn't do that to Sam. Not to his own Carrot Top. Unlike Adam, Rogan believed in being fair with a woman—particularly a woman like Sam, who was already vulnerable.

Sure, telling her it was over between them might hurt Sam for a little while. But she'd get over it. She was strong. He wished he could say the same for himself.

When he opened the door, he discovered she'd changed out of her uniform into stonewashed jeans that softly gloved her thighs, and a salmon-colored T-shirt. His throat was so tight, he didn't say anything. He didn't think he could.

"It was the women," she said. As she walked through the room, her fingertips caressed a chair, skimmed over the back of the couch. Her gaze seemed to scan the oils on the wall, the picture of a woman lifting her child into her arms, another portrait of an old man looking out to sea. "It was a conspiracy. All these women know each other. They run in the same country club set. They decided Adam had so misused Eileen with that awful prenuptial agreement that someone needed to get back at him. They hoped he would be convicted of robbery."

"They hated him that much?"

She turned. The dark background of the midnight sea behind her turned her into a silhouette. Only her hair, fiery red in any light, seemed alive. Rogan ached to feel his fingers running through those misbehaving Orphan Annie curls again. Just once.

"No, I think they all loved Adam in their own way. Apparently he's right when he claims to be quite a ladies' man. But when his mistresses realized how badly he was using Eileen..." She shrugged. "Odd they weren't equally concerned about being a part of his adultery."

"They play by different rules than you do."

"Very much so."

"What's going to happen to them?"

She shrugged. "It's against the law to file a false police report. They're calling their lawyers now. But given the circumstances, I don't think the penalty will be too severe. It's Eileen I feel sorry for. She sincerely thought Adam was trying to get back together with her. The gifts had all arrived by special messenger—anonymously—sort of the other women's penance or show of solidarity, I suppose. Eileen assumed the jewelry was from Adam. And like a fool, she was planning to take him back."

"Even without throwing baubles at a woman, Adam can be very persuasive."

Rogan drew a deep breath. He needed to end the torture, and end it in a hurry. He was no masochist. No man, however noble, should be asked to endure this kind of pain. The anticipation was killing him.

"Adam's been released?" he asked.

"Yes. I suspect he's home by now."

"Great." Rogan shoved his hands into his pockets for fear his urge to touch Sam would become so powerful he couldn't resist the impulse. "Then I guess that's it. I mean, between you and me."

Sam felt every bit of blood drain from her face, leaving her cheeks cold and stiff. She hadn't known quite what to expect when she'd come here to Rogan's house. Perhaps foolishly she'd hoped for another chance at the golden ring—a fantasy she'd never truly believed would happen—not between the millionaire and the housekeeper's daughter.

"We were hot while it lasted," he added, parking himself nonchalantly on a stool at the breakfast bar. He tipped back his beer and drank deeply.

Her knees suffered a bad case of the trembles. "You've got that right."

"So if you ever need anything, let me know. I'll help you out."

"I'll certainly keep that in mind." She wasn't going to beg. No way. That he had slipped past her defenses after all these years was somehow amazing. And yet she'd known she was vulnerable to this one particular man in a way she'd never been to another. And that bothered the hell out of her.

She took a few steps toward the door but before the first tear could spill over, she turned and raised her chin. "I want you to know that I grew up wanting to get married, have a family and a husband who would come home every night. He'd have an ordinary job, and maybe we wouldn't be rich, but he'd be there for the kids. He'd be there for me. Then I did a really stupid thing. When I was thirteen I fell in love with you. I thought sure I'd get over it. I tried, dammit, I honestly did." The lights in the room blurred, refracting in the moisture that filled her eyes.

"But you showed up again, and I knew it was hopeless. I hadn't outgrown you at all. And now, Rogan Prescott, you've ruined me for anyone else." She sniffed and tried to ignore the aching, burning press of tears in her eyes. Fought them desperately. "I really hate you for that."

## Chapter Thirteen

"I'm not crying." Sam scrubbed at the accumulated dirt and grime in the bathroom sink. The only time she ever cleaned house was when she was upset. And she was upset now. She had been since Rogan told her to get lost, three excruciatingly painful days ago.

"Then how come you've got really red eyes?"

Sam clenched her teeth. Marilyn Justice was the most persistent woman she had ever known. "Because I have an allergy."

"Yeah, right. Must be you're allergic to that hunk you've been hanging around with."

"I don't want to talk about him."

"You fell for him that hard, huh?"

Sam blew out a sigh. There was no use pretending, not with her friend. "I didn't know it would hurt so much."

"Yeah, tell me about it. I swear there ought to be a vaccination women could take so we wouldn't make such fools of ourselves. Love? Ha! None of 'em are worth it."

"He warned me it couldn't be forever." Sam

sniffed and swiped halfheartedly at the chrome fixtures. "I should have taken him at his word."

"At least that makes him better than most. He didn't lie to you."

No, Sam was the one who had lied to Rogan. Not that he'd wasted much time finding another date when he'd discovered she'd deceived him. Prescott men didn't have to be too forgiving. Instead, women lined up for them to break their hearts.

Her chin trembled and she tugged her lower lip between her teeth. Damn! Rogan had unwittingly broken her heart when she was thirteen. Now she'd let him do it again.

Fisting the cleaning rag, Sam made a determined effort to think of something besides Rogan.

"Look, Marilyn, they've pulled me off of patrol again and I've got another undercover assignment starting tonight."

"More hanging around with the rich and famous, I hope."

"Just the opposite, I'm afraid." As Sam explained her assignment, she realized how little she was looking forward to the next few days—or rather the nights. But, with luck, she'd be able to keep her mind off of Rogan. "Kind of keep an eye on things for me, will you?"

Smiling, Marilyn gave Sam a reassuring pat on her arm. "Sure, no problem, hon."

HE'D DONE the right thing.

For the better part of a week Rogan had tried to convince himself that he wasn't the world's worst fool.

He'd played volleyball on the beach with the guys, and lost. He drank beer to forget. It didn't do any good. He couldn't even get a buzz on. He jogged and worked out in his gym until every muscle in his body burned with a fury he hadn't felt since his years playing high school football. Sleep eluded him.

Sam couldn't love him. She was too smart for that. Wasn't she?

He stared at the unopened bottle of beer in his hand.

Damn! He *was* an idiot. Sam never lied unless she had a good reason to, like her job. She *did* love him.

And he'd hurt her—far worse than he had ever intended.

Slamming the bottle down on the counter, he grabbed his car keys. He had to see Sam. Now!

He was out the door at a run. The rush-hour traffic was snarled, an accident on Pacific Coast Highway tying everything in a knot. It took him forever to reach Sam's duplex, where he pounded on the door loudly enough to wake the dead.

Marilyn Justice stepped out onto her porch, her expression not exactly welcoming. "Sam's not home."

"Do you know when she'll be back?"

"She shows up at odd hours. She's on another undercover assignment."

Rogan bit back a choice swear word. "Do you have any idea where? I've got to see her."

Marilyn eyed him suspiciously. "I'm not so sure Sam wants to see you. For the last couple of days, she's claimed she was having trouble with her allergies. You know, her eyes were all red and swollen, and she had the sniffles. Funny thing is, I've never known Sam to have any problem with allergies before.'' She gave him an accusing look. "You wouldn't know anything about that, would you?''

Yeah, he did, and he felt guilty as hell that he'd caused Sam such misery. "Maybe I can find the cure if you can tell me where Sam is.''

Marilyn studied him at some length. She was a pretty woman, though there was a shadow of both wariness and weariness in her eyes. Ever so slightly, her lips curled with the threat of a smile. "She said something about working Sunset Boulevard.''

"Working?''

"She's undercover as a hooker.''

"No!'' Rogan exploded. He couldn't believe such stupidity.

Without even saying goodbye, he turned on his heel and raced to his car.

He made it to Sunset Boulevard in record time. While the street wasn't exactly empty, it was too early for much action. He cruised slowly past parked cars, peering at the pedestrians, particularly the females who were loitering near corners. Damn, he was really out of his element now.

"Hi, sugar,'' a woman dressed in a short leather skirt called from the sidewalk. "Wanta have some fun?''

He pulled to the curb and rolled down the passenger window. "I'm looking for a woman—''

"Sugar, you have certainly come to the right place!''

Damned if he didn't blush. "No, you don't understand. I'm looking for a particular woman. A redhead—''

"Trust me, babyface. There's nothing a redhead could do for you that I can't."

"Thanks anyway." He waved her off and accelerated back into the flow of traffic. The street was tawdry, the bright lights unable to mask the seamier side of life. The dangerous side. "Ah, Sam..." The need to protect her from any and all danger rose up in him like a living thing, filling his chest and closing his throat. He could hardly breathe.

He *had* to find Sam.

He cruised up and down the boulevard for hours. His stomach growled but he didn't want to take the chance of missing her by taking a break to eat something. In spite of the car's air conditioner, sweat formed along his spine and under his arms. Though he hadn't prayed in years, he sent up a plea to keep Sam safe. He knew he'd never survive if something bad happened to her.

When he finally spotted her, Sam was talking to a guy in a BMW sedan. She was dressed in leotards that had to be painted on, every sleek line of her gorgeous legs emphasized by the tight fit and made to look sinfully long.

Rogan roared up beside the BMW, slammed on the brakes and leapt out of his Bronco. He walked around to the front of the car and glared through the windshield at the driver, a big hulking guy with a pockmarked face.

"She's not available," he growled. "Get lost."

He barely managed to step up onto the curb before the BMW sped off into the night.

Sam rolled her eyes and sighed. "It's all right, guys," she said into the hidden mike attached to her bra. "This one's harmless." Though the fire in Rogan's eyes might suggest otherwise to a casual observer.

She could all but hear a sigh of relief from her backup in the van a few hundred feet down the street.

"Rogan, what in heaven's name are you doing here?"

He hooked his arm through hers. "I'm taking you home, that's what I'm doing."

She balked. "No way. I'm working—"

"If you don't want him, sweetie," crooned one of the street ladies who was working the same corner, "I sure do."

"You're going to blow my cover," Sam snarled. "Get out of here."

"Not without you."

*Impossible man!* Arrogant. Stubborn. A man whose greatest talent was breaking a woman's heart.

Sam spoke into the mike. "Bobby, I've got to take care of this. It won't take long." Then, in a movement she hoped appeared natural, she reached up under her tight-fitting halter top and disconnected the mike.

"So?" she asked, her voice intentionally nasal and loud enough to be heard by anyone nearby. "Ya wanna rent a room? Or are we gonna do it in your car?"

He yanked her toward the Bronco, but she had some small sense of gratification that Rogan's natural ruddy color had drained from his face.

"Rogan, you're going to break my arm," she complained, stumbling as he shoved her into the passenger seat.

"It'd serve you right," he mumbled in response.

It didn't take him long to get around to the driver's side. With a jerk, he shifted into gear and sped down the boulevard, wheeling right at the first street he came to. Abruptly, he halted the Bronco at the curb. He turned toward her, and Sam could practically see steam coming out of his ears, he was so furious.

"Do you have any idea how dangerous it is for a woman to walk the streets in this part of town? You could get killed, for God's sake."

Calmly she said, "I had plenty of backup on hand, if you'd taken a minute or two to look around."

"I don't give a damn about your backup."

In a deceptively swift movement, he pulled her to him. Before Sam had a chance to object, she was in his arms and he was covering her face with hot, frantic kisses.

"Rogan, you've got to stop." *She* had to stop before she succumbed to the sheer pleasure of his touch, his kiss, the scent of him that she'd missed so much.

"I'm not going to stop until you say you'll marry me."

The earth ground to an absolute halt, its rotation ceased, and Sam felt sure she was going to spin off into space. "Marry?" The word was little more than a whisper—or maybe a plea that dreams could come true.

"You got that damn straight. I'm not going to have you wandering around masquerading as who-knows-what just so you can catch a crook or two. I want you home where I can keep track of you and keep you safe."

Slowly, the world began to spin again. Painfully, she shoved away from Rogan. Her jaw taut, she said,

"This is my job. Catching bad guys is what I'm sup- posed to do." Though most of the women working the streets could scarcely be described as hardened criminals. In fact, she'd had the urge to take the younger girls to somewhere like Chandler House where they could start over again. But that wasn't her job. Not tonight.

"You don't have to be a cop anymore. You don't have to work at all. I'll take care of you. You won't lack for anything. I swear it."

He didn't get it. Maybe when she was eight and he'd climbed up the tree to sit beside her, Sam had needed someone to rescue her. Or when he'd fixed the tires on her bike. But that wasn't true now. She could take care of herself and wouldn't have it any other way. If there was anything in this world that she did need, it was a man who would love her just as she was—freckles and all—and would always be there beside her.

The way Rogan ran hot and cold, she'd never be able to trust him. And she just couldn't deal with that. What she wanted was his love—not to be rescued from the life she'd chosen, however frustrated and unhappy she was with it at the moment.

"I'm sorry, Rogan. I'm not a stray puppy that's been abandoned. If you want to rescue somebody you should hang around Chandler House where you could do some real good. I'm sure there are a lot of kids there who could use your help."

A frown lowered his dark eyebrows. "You're turn- ing me down?"

She swallowed hard. "I'm turning you down." Which didn't mean she wasn't tempted. In fact, her heart was beating like a tom-tom, threatening to go on the warpath with her good reason.

"But I could give you everything in the world you want. I've got millions. You want a bigger house? It's yours. You want to travel to Europe? I'll book our flight right now. Whatever—"

"No, Rogan."

"But you said you love me." He looked genuinely perplexed.

She gently caressed his whisker-roughened cheek. "The way I look at things, love doesn't come with a price tag. Thanks anyway. I appreciate your asking."

He looked so totally stunned, Sam decided she'd walk the short distance back to the boulevard. She didn't want to be responsible for Rogan's having an accident. And she needed to get out of there before she had any second thoughts—and before her eyes turned into salt-flavored fountains.

Strangely, her legs had trouble obeying her command to exit the car. Then, when her feet hit the sidewalk, her knees wobbled.

As she reached the corner, she glanced over her shoulder. The taillights of the Bronco were just vanishing out of sight in the opposite direction. The hollow feel of regret filled her chest and she had the urge to go running after him.

She'd just turned down her very first proposal, a proposal from the only man she had ever loved. Maybe she ought to head directly to the police department shrink and let him straighten her out.

But her mother had loved Sam's father, so much so, she'd rarely smiled after he'd abandoned them. Sam remembered that bleak joylessness. She wasn't sure she could endure that again, not if her own heart was the one shattered by infidelity. And without love...

THE NEXT NIGHT she was on the street again. Her job was a dual one. First to gain the trust of the women who worked there and then to find out who was preying on them. In the past month, three women had been found dead. This wasn't a job Sam particularly relished, but someone had to do it. None of these women deserved to die. She could only wish someone had been around when they were young to help them make a different choice.

Cocking her hip, she smiled at the passing motorists. Any one of them could be a killer.

Just as a Jeep cruised by, the driver inspecting the merchandise, Sam became aware of the heavy click of high heels on the sidewalk behind her. She turned to look over her shoulder and her jaw dropped.

The creature she saw wore a walnut-brown wig with garish streaks of silver-blond highlights. Makeup had been applied thickly, and a shocking red shade of lipstick outlined a familiar mouth. The clothing selection looked as if it had come from a costume shop; skintight leotards did nothing to disguise muscular legs, and a striped halter top was accentuated by what could only be a matching pair of fully ripe grapefruit. The four-inch heels made him look like he was walking on stilts.

Sam choked on a laugh. Or maybe it was a sob. "Rogan? What on earth—"

"Hope you don't mind sharing your corner, sweetie," he said in a falsetto voice. "Don't you know, business has been so slow down at my end of the street.''

"You can't stay here!" she snapped.

"Hey, Big Mama," one of the other ladies said. "What's going down?"

Rogan affected a twirl of his wrist. Given his hairy arm, it wasn't a very feminine gesture. "Don't mind me, darlings. Plenty of room for everyone, I always say."

"Please, Rogan, I'm working. You can't—"

"I won't get in your way," he said under his breath. "I'm just making sure nothing bad happens to you. You never know what kind of creep might try to pick you up."

Sam wanted to scream. The man was insane! "That's the whole idea. We're trying to catch a murderer."

Even beneath the thick layer of makeup, Sam could see Rogan's face pale.

"All the more reason why I'm going to stay right here next to you."

Desperately trying to figure out a way to get rid of Rogan, she glanced down the street toward the van that contained her backup. To her dismay, two of the most unlikely looking hookers she'd ever seen were coming in her direction down the sidewalk.

"No!" she wailed. This couldn't be happening to her. Her fledgling police career was about to go down the tubes.

"Hi, you two," Eileen said brightly. She was wearing a low-cut silver Spandex jumpsuit that stretched over every curve like an extra layer of skin. "We had a terrible time finding a place to park but we're so glad we found you."

"Isn't this fun?" Agatha said with equal enthusiasm. "I never knew wearing leather would attract so much attention." When she smoothed her short skirt, the brim of her leather hat dipped to a come-hither angle.

"You people can't do this," Sam protested.

"Oh, but we were worried about you, my dear. Rogan said you might be in danger."

Sam gritted her teeth. "I'm not in danger. Honestly, I'm not." Or she hadn't been until an assortment of Prescotts had arrived, drawing undo attention to the undercover operation.

"I didn't know they were coming, too," Rogan assured her. "I needed to use some of Eileen's makeup and I guess I sort of let the cat out of the bag."

A car rolled by the corner, the windows down, the trio of men inside hooting at them. Another driver honked. It was hard to know which one of this odd cast of characters was attracting the most attention. Sam felt sure it wasn't her.

One of the real working girls whom Sam had befriended planted her fists on her hips and glared at Sam. "Hey, what's going on? This is *my* corner. I only said *you* could hang out here. You're messing up my business."

"Look, I'm sorry. These are my friends—"

"What charming earrings, my dear," Agatha said to the hooker. She fingered the gaudy, dangling earrings. "So unusual. Are they real? I do so love real diamonds."

Sam choked. Surely Agatha wasn't planning to snatch that garish pair of rhinestone earrings.

The young woman beamed at the compliment. "You like 'em? I picked 'em up real cheap at this swap meet I went to about a year ago. The johns really go for—"

"Please! All of you." Sam was very near the breaking point. "Bobby! Help me!" she called to her partner, who was listening at the other end of her hidden microphone. "Get these people out of here."

An engine started. Tires squealed. The van roared up to the corner and the doors slid open. Three men, all wearing Police-emblazoned windbreakers, leapt out of the vehicle.

Startled, Agatha's hand flew to her chest. "Oh, my—"

"Vice!" The resident hooker shouted a warning and took off running down the sidewalk.

"My, aren't these gentlemen handsome," Eileen murmured appreciatively.

Rogan didn't budge. He simply looked smug. "Looks like you'll be getting off work early this evening, Sam. You wanna go out for a bite to eat?" When she simply glared at him, he said, "You aren't going to tell me *this* is why you became a cop, are you?" His gesture took in the seediness of the street.

No, she couldn't tell him that. But she *was* going to kill him! With her bare hands, if she could—right after she found a way to convince her partners not to arrest Rogan and his overdressed cohorts for interfering with a police investigation.

WITH CONSIDERABLE EFFORT, Sam eluded Rogan's pursuit for the next several days. She didn't know why he was being so darn persistent. She'd made it abundantly clear she didn't want to be rescued—by him or anyone else.

She ignored the messages he left on her answering machine; flowers arrived daily, usually with an expensive bauble tucked inside—a diamond bracelet or a set of earrings. She returned the jewelry. But in spite of herself, she kept the flowers. Their sweet scent filled the duplex, taunting her with dreams she didn't dare try to claim as reality.

Naturally she'd been pulled off the Sunset Boulevard case. Given the scene the Prescott Masqueraders had made on the street, she wouldn't be any use undercover on that assignment.

Instead, with a spiteful gleam in his eyes, Garcia had sent her back to patrol duty.

Oddly, she hated it. They'd arrested one purse snatcher twice in as many days. He'd been back on the street before they even finished the paperwork. As far as Sam could tell, she wasn't making one whit of difference. This was *not* what she had envisioned being a police officer would mean, nor did she feel the memory of Dee and Marcia was being well served.

Feeling frustrated and out of sorts at the end of her shift one evening, she heard a knock. Half expecting to find Rogan parked on her porch, she yanked open the door, fully ready to give him an earful about how he'd ruined her career—which at the moment she didn't care a fig about anyway.

"Eileen?" she questioned, surprised to find Rogan's sister-in-law standing there.

"I hope I'm not interrupting anything. If you're

busy—"

"No, not at all." Sam opened the door wider. Outfitted in a two-piece dress with pearl buttons and wide shoulder pads, Eileen looked like she'd just come from her job as an upscale receptionist—or had stepped right out of a fashion magazine. "I was trying to decide whether to make a salad for dinner out of two-week-old, slightly blackened lettuce, or open a can of soup."

Eileen wrinkled her nose. "The soup sounds safer."

"You're right."

Her gaze slid around the living room, taking in the simple furnishings. "This is nice. Cozy."

"It's hardly what you're used to."

With an indifferent shrug, Eileen chose the comfortable chair by the bookcase and sat down. "Having a lot of money is highly overrated, as you may have guessed."

"I've never considered it a priority," Sam conceded. "Though the absence of money isn't a whole lot of fun, either."

"How do you feel about love?"

Sam's heart spasmed. "I'm all for it," she replied cautiously.

Eileen's fingers curved gracefully over the end of the armrest, her nails perfectly manicured and polished in a striking shade of pink. "Then is there some other reason why you turned down Rogan's proposal?"

"He doesn't love me, Eileen." Sam's throat tightened around the truth. "Just like he does with everyone else, all Rogan has wanted to do from the beginning is rescue me. He acts out a game of gentleman bountiful—with you, Aunt Agatha, all those artists he supports. Even Goofus. From the beginning, he wanted to reform me and then marry me off to one of his wealthy friends. His proposal was no more than a last-ditch effort to save me from myself.''

''Really? From what I've seen, Rogan has been brought to his knees by a bad case of lovesickness.''

''I suppose that's why as soon as I was out of the picture, he went out with that Heidi person.''

''I didn't say I could totally explain *any* man. I don't suppose a woman can hope to do that. But trust me on this, Sam. Rogan has fallen for you about as hard as a man can.''

Reluctant to accept Eileen's version of the situation at face value, Sam frowned. Rogan's own words came back to her. *I'm not a forever kind of guy.* How could she risk believing otherwise?

''The poor man believes he can't make a commitment,'' Eileen said, ''and that's why he's never given marriage a try. But think about it, Sam. Have you ever, *ever* known anyone who was more loyal, more *faithful* to everyone he's ever known? Including Adam, who doesn't deserve one ounce of his loyalty?''

Sam shook her head. ''I don't know. If only I could be sure he loved me.''

''Why don't you flat out ask him, Sam? In all the years I've known Rogan, I've never once known him to lie. I think it's his dogged loyalty that sets Rogan apart from any other man I've ever met. Certainly any other Prescott.''

But could he be loyal to her?

SAM GAVE CONSIDERABLE thought to Eileen's comments all through a sleepless night and on through the better part of the next day while she was on patrol, riding shotgun in a black-and-white with a new partner.

The sharp crackle of the radio and the disembodied voice of the dispatcher brought her out of her reverie.

''Units Seven and Nineteen. Two-eleven in progress. Provide backup at Vons Market, corner of Midland and Sepulveda. Code Three.''

Adrenaline pumping, Sam grabbed the mike and responded to dispatch that they were on the way. Nick, her partner, shot her a grin as he flicked the switch for the siren. The radio was alive with other units en route and requests for more to secure the area.

''Sounds like a big one going down,'' Nick said, looking pleased as punch to get into the action. ''You can bet there were customers in the store, and now they're hostages.''

In contrast to Nick's enthusiasm, fear snaked into Sam's midsection. She might be new to this but she'd been on the force long enough to know—outside of domestic disputes—hostage situations were the most dangerous of all.

When they arrived at their destination five minutes later there were four units already on site, and the looky-loos were crowding the perimeter of the crime scene. At least two holdup men had fled into the grocery store after they'd tried to rob an armored car delivering cash. They were armed, dangerous, and had already clipped a guard with a wild shot as they went inside.

No one knew for sure how many hostages were being held or what the holdup men looked like.

Civilians had little sense about the potential danger in a volatile hostage situation. Sam wished they'd all go home and watch the whole thing on television. The whirl of helicopters overhead was a sure sign the local channels were getting a bird's-eye view to be played back on the evening news.

Moving cautiously, Sam exited the car and walked toward a protected spot at the side of the building. She scanned the parking area and then the onlookers.

"Damn!"

Of all people, Rogan was standing smack in the middle of the crowd. How the devil had he gotten here before she had—unless he'd been monitoring police frequencies and keeping track of her, she realized with an internal groan.

At that very moment a woman came running out of the store with a baby in her arms.

"Don't shoot," she cried hysterically. "I'm not one of them. Please don't shoot. My baby!" She stumbled and fell to her knees, sobbing, and didn't seem able to get up.

Sam's heart lurched at the sight of them.

She knew they were in danger unless they got out of the line of fire in a hurry. From where she was standing at the corner of the building, she judged that if she moved quickly she could get to the woman, get her to her feet, and get her to safety without making herself a target. She hoped.

Knowing there was no time to delay, she made for the woman at a dead run.

"Sam, don't!" It was Rogan's voice she heard shouting at her, not her partner's.

She reached the woman's side and, an instant later, so had Rogan.

"Get out of here!" she commanded.

His face a taut mask, he ignored her. "Not till you're out of danger."

Together, they helped the woman to her feet.

That's when the first shot was fired.

Rogan straightened, his eyes wide.

All hell broke loose then. Police officers descended on the store from all directions. The baby started crying. The woman screamed.

Sam raced the mother and child out of the line of fire.

When she turned back to see what had happened behind her, her stomach nearly changed places with her heart.

Rogan was sprawled face-down on the sidewalk, a stain of bright red spreading across the back of his shirt.

Her scream was an echo of the past—Dee and Marcia, lying on the ground, blood oozing from their bodies in a grotesque pattern that somehow had been Sam's fault. The memory was so vivid, she gagged.

And now she'd lost Rogan, too.

## Chapter Fourteen

The smell of antiseptic lodged at the back of Sam's throat.

"You lost it today, Officer Sterling." Her captain said it sympathetically but she knew he was thinking she never should have joined the force.

Right now, Sam was in total agreement. Dear God, if Rogan died because of her...

"You could have gotten yourself killed. If that civilian hadn't been between you and the shooter, it might be *you* having surgery now. Or I could be down in the morgue picking up your personal effects."

Sam recognized that. Oddly, she was aware her captain's anger was mostly residual fear for one of his officers. That didn't help her appreciably. Rogan had foolishly risked his life to protect her—to rescue her. And now she wasn't sure what she'd do if he died because of doing something so utterly stupid.

And heroic.

His actions had saved the woman and her baby, too. Without his help, in spite of what Sam had thought in the heat of the moment, she might not have been able to get the mother to her feet.

Maybe she wasn't such a good cop after all. Maybe she was too ruled by her emotions. In that regard, she and Rogan were a lot alike—determined to *save* people. In her case it was the memory of Dee and Marcia that had driven her all these years. What motivated Rogan? she wondered.

Unable to sit still, Sam paced the waiting room and gnawed on her lower lip. She fought a Niagara Falls of tears that threatened. If only someone would come out of those swinging doors and tell them what was going on.

Across the room, Agatha and Eileen sat huddled together giving each other comfort. A family, Sam mused, however dysfunctional and eccentric some of the members might be. Rogan was loyal to every one of them. In return, they were faithful to him.

In her heart of hearts, she knew she'd give her soul to claim kinship by marriage to the same family fidelity. Well, maybe not to Adam, she mentally corrected with a hurried second thought.

Just then the doors to the operating area swung open, driving all other thoughts from Sam's mind. A lanky doctor dressed in surgical greens appeared and walked directly toward her. She held her breath.

"Mr. Prescott said I wouldn't be able to miss you. All I had to do was look for a Carrot Top." He smiled gently.

Myriad emotions pressed at the sudden tears in her eyes. At least Rogan was talking. Surely that was a good sign. But her throat felt so tight, so terribly raw and painful, she couldn't form a coherent question.

"He's a very lucky man," the doctor said, apparently aware that she was unable to speak. "The bullet did amazingly little damage. It didn't even graze any vital organs. Our largest concern has been the concussion he sustained when he fell and hit his head. Now that he's talking, we suspect his recovery will progress quite rapidly."

Sam's chin trembled. Without giving it much thought, she took the surgeon's hand and squeezed tightly. "Thank you, doctor."

"He's in recovery now and it may be a couple of hours before he'll be moved to a room. But he's very much awake, and determined to see you, even if he has to come out here himself. I think it would be better, in this case, if you'd go to him."

Seeing no reason to debate the issue, Sam hurried through the swinging doors.

A HALF-DOZEN PATIENTS lay on gurneys in the recovery room; nurses bustled around checking blood pressures and taking pulses. The doctor led Sam to Rogan's side.

Fighting a new onset of tears, Sam stroked his cheek, his whiskers rough and familiar against her palm, then she swept back a lock of hair that had fallen across his forehead. Her fingers trembled. In spite of being linked to an IV and oxygen, his color was good, his flesh warm and alive to the touch.

His eyes fluttered open. A half smile curled his lips as recognition lit his beautiful blue eyes.

"You idiot," she whispered lovingly, her chest tight with relief. "You scared me half to death."

"Now you know how *I* feel," he said, his voice raspy and a little unsteady, "knowing you're out there playing cops and robbers."

Was that true? Did he truly care as much about her as she did about him?

It wasn't possible that anyone could love a man more than she loved Rogan. Or be so furious that he had needlessly risked his neck. "If your skull wasn't so thick, you might have been seriously hurt."

He licked his lips. "Thickheadedness runs in the family."

"Didn't it occur to you the gunman might take a shot at you?"

"I wanted to protect you, and you went running out there—"

"I had on a bulletproof vest. You might as well have been naked. What you need, Rogan, is a keeper."

His lips twitched. "Know anyone who wants the job?"

Sam hesitated. Old insecurities and fears were hard to discard even in the face of such powerful emotions. For so many years she'd questioned that a man like Rogan could be faithful to a woman. But maybe all along she'd been wrong.

"Maybe you better not commit just yet," he said. "This little escapade might cost me my job."

She frowned and touched him again, unable to stop reassuring herself that he was alive. Even if he was hallucinating. "Your job?"

"Yeah. I'm suppose to start work at Chandler House next week. The executive director found a more secure job with another agency, so to save money the board hired me as his replacement." His grin was a little lopsided. "They're paying me a dollar a year."

"A dollar?" she echoed dumbly. Why would Rogan even want a job, much less the dollar they were paying him?

"Tell you the truth, it's the first honest job I've ever had. Can't expect to get paid much."

"No, I suppose not." Given Rogan's bank account, the money wasn't important. But she could tell having a *job* was. He looked so darn proud of himself, even though, in his drugged condition, his grin was a little lopsided, maybe that's what had been wrong all along. He'd simply lacked a sense of direction. "You'll be wonderful as the director. I'm sure they'll give you a raise after you prove yourself. Maybe even double your salary," she teased.

"'Course, I have hopes of expanding the programs at Chandler House." He licked his lips again and a nurse handed her a moist cotton swab for him to suck on. "They've got good activities for the guys, but not much for the girls. I thought maybe I could start a sports program for them, beginning with volleyball. *If* I could find the right coach."

Her heart leapt. "I see."

"Couldn't pay her much."

"A dollar a year?"

"Something like that. It wouldn't have to be a full-time job, if she had something else she wanted to do. Of course, helping those girls who are at risk might be just as useful as, say..." A slight shrug made him wince. "Being a cop."

Sam thought he might be right about that, particularly considering the frustration she'd experienced recently, and how much she'd truly enjoyed her summer jobs during college as a YMCA counselor and as a part-time coach. Maybe her memory of Dee and Marcia would be better served if she pursued a different career. That thought both excited and intrigued her. Until now she'd held on to her belief that police work was the way she could make a difference as tenaciously as Rogan had maintained his conviction that he wasn't a forever kind of guy. It was entirely possible they were both wrong.

"What if this woman you have in mind is independently wealthy?" she asked.

"You know some lady who is about to get rich?"

"I might if a particular man I know would propose again. And say that he loved her."

The entire recovery room seemed to go still. As far as Sam could tell, the nurses stopped midstride; patients held their breaths. Even the monitors seemed to halt between beats. Or maybe it was Sam whose entire awareness teetered on the brink between hope and despair.

"Haven't I mentioned that?" he asked.

"No, you haven't."

Rogan felt suddenly light-headed, as if somebody had turned up the oxygen. And scared, really scared. More even than when that bullet had slammed into his back. He wanted Sam to be his so much, he could taste it. If she turned him down now...

"I love you, Sam. More than any man has a right. I'm sorry I didn't tell you before."

Her heart started up its cadence again, swelling inside her chest. "Not too long ago you told me it was over. What changed your mind?"

"I'd never had a woman love me before. My

money, yeah. The good times, sure. But not *me*. Took me a while to believe it was true.''

"It is, sweetheart. I love you more than I can say. I have for a very long time."

Taking her hand, he tugged her down toward him. "Everything I have, everything I own, is yours, Carrot Top. All you have to do is marry me."

"All I want is forever, Rogan. Can you promise me that?"

"Count on it."

When her lips touched his, Sam tasted his promise and knew it was true. There was no other man with a greater capacity for loyalty; he'd demonstrated that attribute in a thousand different ways. That made Rogan Prescott the absolutely perfect man for her.

How strange she hadn't realized that sooner.

"I want kids, you know," she told him, her fingers threading through his hair.

"Great." With a sappy grin that appeared to be half pleasure and half pain medication, he said, "Could you give me a couple of days before we get started on that project?"

She knew she'd be willing to wait a lifetime for Rogan, or even longer, if that's what it took. He'd stolen her heart a long time ago. Now she was going to put a ball and chain on the thief, and never let him escape.

 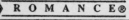
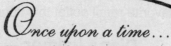

# And the Winner Is...
# You!

...when you pick up these great titles
from our new promotion at your
favorite retail outlet this June!

**Diana Palmer**
*The Case of the Mesmerizing Boss*

**Betty Neels**
*The Convenient Wife*

**Annette Broadrick**
*Irresistible*

**Emma Darcy**
*A Wedding to Remember*

**Rachel Lee**
*Lost Warriors*

**Marie Ferrarella**
*Father Goose*

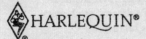 

Look us up on-line at: http://www.romance.net ATWI397-R

*It's hot...and it's out of control!*

Beginning this spring, Temptation turns up the
*heat.* Look for these bold, provocative,
*ultra*sexy books!

**#629 OUTRAGEOUS**
by Lori Foster (April 1997)

**#639 RESTLESS NIGHTS**
by Tiffany White (June 1997)

**#649 NIGHT RHYTHMS**
by Elda Minger (Sept. 1997)

***BLAZE:* Red-hot reads—only from**

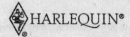

# HE SAID

♥

# SHE SAID

Explore the mystery of male/female communication in this extraordinary new book from two of your favorite Harlequin authors.

Jasmine Cresswell and Margaret St. George bring you the exciting story of two romantic adversaries—each from their own point of view!

DEV'S STORY. CATHY'S STORY.
As he sees it. As she sees it.
Both sides of the story!

The heat is definitely on, and these two can't stay out of the kitchen!

Don't miss **HE SAID, SHE SAID.**
Available in July wherever Harlequin books are sold.

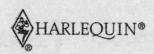

He changes diapers, mixes formula and
tells wonderful bedtime stories—he's

# Mr. Mom

Three totally different stories of sexy, single
heroes each raising another man's child...
from three of your favorite authors:

**MEMORIES OF THE PAST**
by Carole Mortimer

**THE MARRIAGE TICKET**
by Sharon Brondos

**TELL ME A STORY**
by Dallas Schulze

Available this June wherever
Harlequin and Silhouette books are sold.

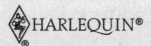 

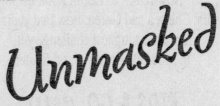